Sauce for the Goose

NOVELS BY ROBERT CAMPBELL

The Jimmy Flannery Series
The Junkyard Dog
The 600 Pound Gorilla
Hip-Deep in Alligators
The Cat's Meow
Thinning the Turkey Herd
Nibbled to Death by Ducks
The Gift Horse's Mouth
In a Pig's Eye
Sauce for the Goose

The Whistler Series
In La-La Land We Trust
Alice in La-La Land
Sweet La-La Land
The Wizard of La-La Land

The Jake Hatch Series
Plugged Nickel
Red Cent

Other Crime Novels
Honor
Juice
Boneyards

Writing as R. Wright Campbell
The Spy Who Sat and Waited
Circus Couronne
Where Pigeons Go to Die
Killer of Kings
Malloy's Subway
Fat Tuesday

Writing as F.G. Clinton
The Tin Cop

ROBERT CAMPBELL

SAUCE FOR THE GOOSE

THE MYSTERIOUS PRESS

Published by Warner Books

A Time Warner Company

C.1 8.95
18.7.95

First published in Great Britain in 1994 by Hodder and Stoughton Ltd, London.

Copyright © 1994 Robert Campbell

 Mysterious Press books are published by Warner Books, Inc.,
1271 Avenue of the Americas, New York, NY 10020.

 A Time Warner Company

The Mysterious Press name and logo are registered trademarks of Warner Books, Inc.

Printed in the United States of America

First U.S. printing: August 1995

10 9 8 7 6 5 4 3 2 1

Library of Congress Cataloging-in-Publication Data
Campbell, R. Wright.
      Sauce for the goose / Robert Campbell.
         p.   cm.
      ISBN 0-89296-608-4 (hardcover)
         1. Flannery, Jimmy (Fictitious character)—Fiction.
      2. Politicians—Illinois—Chicago—Fiction. 3. Chicago (Ill.)-
      -Fiction. I. Title.
      PS3553.A4867S28   1994
      813'.54—dc20   94-45318
                                                                  CIP

SAUCE FOR THE GOOSE

1

My name's Jimmy Flannery.

My wife's name is Mary Ellen.

She had a baby the beginning of this year. The baby's name is Kathleen.

Like every new father what ever lived I feel a little lost around the house, the baby being the center of my wife's universe. I can understand that because she's sort of become the center of my universe too, I love her so much, but that don't keep me from missing the way it was when there was just Mary and me, just the two of us.

A baby changes your life more than all the career plans and ideas for the future you can imagine. I mean it ain't like it's a dog what you can tell to go lay down in the corner.

Which, speaking of dogs, my dog, Alfie, ain't made up his mind about the newcomer to the household.

First he was my dog and then he got to be Mary's dog and now it looks like he's making up his mind if he should be Kathleen's dog or maybe be his own dog and take on the responsibility of a pet of his own, which is how I sometimes think he thinks about Kathleen.

It's not that Alfie's exactly fickle, it's just that a dog's very practical and will usually go to the person what can give him the most comfort and affection. On the other hand there's dogs who go where they feel they're most needed, just like some people. So Alfie's making up his mind which way he wants to move. My bet is that he ain't going to be taking on any new responsibilities anytime soon.

The first six months I must have been up twenty times a night because Kathleen would spit the pacifier out of her mouth and start fussing, which activates the baby alert, which activates the speaker in our bedroom. So I'd stumble out of bed and stagger into the nursery, stick the gob-stopper back into her little pink mouth, tuck the blanket in around her little chin and go back to bed where I'd lay and worry about why she was so quiet—crib death and all being so much in the news—until I start dozing off, at which time she spits out the pacifier and we start all over again.

Alfie wakes up every time I wake up, and if I don't wake up quick enough he comes in and paws me until I do.

Which maybe looks like I'm wrong about him taking Kathleen on as a responsibility but which—you examine the situation with an eye which ain't clouded with sentiment—only means he don't want to lose any more sleep listening to a wailing baby than he absolutely has to.

Things are easing off a little now, and sometimes Kathleen even sleeps right on through until six A.M.

That's when I get up to get ready for my job down at the Sewer Department where I'm an inspector. Being an inspector means that I don't have to be down in the pipes every day but only now and then.

Also I accepted the position—unpaid—of committeeman in the Twenty-seventh Ward where we live. I been a precinct captain for the Democratic party for about fifteen years so I know the ward like I know the palm of my hand and—like they say—my time had come to step up to the head of the line or take a walk. Not that most people think it means a hell of a lot any more, the old Machine being rusted and busted the way everybody says it is.

In the good old/bad old days the Regular Democratic Party Organization ran on patronage. If a man needed a job and the Party gave him a job? . . . it expected his vote. A man worked for the Party, he was rewarded with a job. There was some jobs like the one Kippy Kerner had down at the County Building before his retirement where he came in every morning to see that the steam engineer had adjusted the valves on the furnaces. The comedians say that Kippy passed away last year from the hard work of doing nothing, but what they don't know is that Kippy busted up both legs back in '59, falling off a bridge he was maintaining, trying to save his buddy. He had workmen's compensation and health insurance, so he wasn't hurting all that much financially, except he was losing his pride, what with having nothing to do, so the old mayor give him a little something. Which Kippy took even though it meant losing part of his workmen's comp. He wasn't looking for a handout or a free ride. He was down there making sure those valves was checked winter and summer.

It could be true that another person of my acquaintance is sitting in the butter tub, but even if Billy Swinarski don't seem to be doing much, sitting outside the city treasurer's office—which, incidentally, has a big sign on the door—directing people to the city treasurer's office, he's always got a cheerful word and on a gloomy day that can count for a lot.

I got my own job in the sewers through connections but I always worked hard at it, and if you think a job in the sewers is a gift, well maybe you should have another look. Though I ain't complaining. I'm just pointing out that if you don't give jobs to your friends, who you going give them to, your enemies?

Jobs has always been a political issue.

Back in 1947, the Party nominated and elected Martin "Snow White" Kennelly, a reform candidate, for reasons having to do with gambling and a perception of public corruption involving the incumbent too devious and complicated to explain. They figured they could keep him on a leash, but he got away from them; eight years later he goes ahead and tosses twelve thousand patronage jobs into the civil service system. So that's how the party turned their backs on Kennelly and ran Richard J. Daley for mayor. The rest—like they say—is history.

It was business as usual for a while until the

Shankman ruling in federal court supposedly ended patronage and nepotism in Chicago forever.

Another thing you could think about is the old remark about how nepotism is only bad when you're not the one getting the benefit of it.

So, anyway, maybe you don't see as many loyal precinct workers walking the streets and knocking on doors, helping their neighbors and getting out the vote on election day, who got jobs down at City Hall running the automatic elevators or chauffeuring aldermen around.

The way we do politics is changing just like everything else. So what you see is lawyers, bankers and wheeler-dealers spreading the grease around, which is then used on television ads to sell the people on the candidate of their choice. These are the men who end up handing out the deals for floating city bond issues and the contracts for consulting on this or that.

Also, anybody who knows anything about patronage and clout, knows that there's always a mousehole, an angle, a back door.

Just the other night, Janet Canarias, the lipstick lesbian who stole the Twenty-seventh's aldermanic seat from the Regular Democratic Organization, stops by to chew the fat in her storefront office, which she lets me use to see my constituents on Monday nights, and asks me did I read the editorial about the mayor in the *Wall Street Journal*?

"I don't ever read the *Wall Street Journal*," I says. "I've got no investments."

"It's not exclusively about business, you know," she

says. "They have some very interesting editorials and commentaries about politics."

"Well, one way you look at it, politics is business and business is politics."

"That's right," she says. "People vote their pocketbooks more than they vote anything else. That and making sure city services like garbage pickup and snow removal get done."

She's referring to when Bilandic lost the mayoral election to Jane Byrne back in '79 when he does such a lousy job getting the snow off the streets and the public transportation running smooth in that awful winter. Which then sets Byrne up to lose to Harold Washington because she don't understand how it was the time for her to politically embrace the blacks and Hispanics and gays instead of jumping back into bed with the old back-room boys after kicking their asses the way she did. Which, in a curious way, teaches the new mayor the lessons he needs to get elected after Washington dies of a heart attack.

"Can I get you a cup of coffee?" I asks.

"That would be nice," she says. "You mind if I take off my shoes?"

"Why should I mind? It's your office. Go ahead, make yourself comfortable."

She kicks off her heels and stretches her legs—which are very long and much appreciated even by men who don't approve of her lifestyle—out on the desk, wrapping her skirt around her thighs in a very ladylike way.

I bring her a cup of coffee, black, no sugar, the way

she likes it and sit down behind her desk with a cup of
my own.

"What did the *Wall Street Journal* have to say?" I
asks, getting her back to her original remark.

"They spent a whole editorial praising the mayor for
planning to turn over selected city services to the private sector."

"Well, so far they ain't talking about much," I says.
"Animal Control and some of the Consumer Information and Complaints."

"That's just the beginning."

"What makes you say that?"

She taps the side of her nose.

"Fish?" I says.

"Things aren't always what they seem."

"You got any evidence of a conspiracy, anything like
that?" I asks.

She shakes her head no.

"Just a feeling at the back of my neck."

"So, you need any help with the feeling, all you got
to do is ask."

"Even if it gives the Party a black eye?"

"It couldn't be anything small," I says.

"I know that, Jimmy. I'm not out there swinging
an axe anymore. I know how to pick and choose my
battles. It's funny how you start out thinking you're
going to sweep the streets clean of every little bit of
garbage, then you're happy if you can just keep it
from becoming a flood, maybe keep your own street
tidy."

"That's the way it's supposed to work, everybody

taking care of their own mess, minding their own business and letting everybody else mind theirs."

"It's drawing the line that's so hard to do, Jimmy," she says. "It's drawing that damn line."

2

I used to walk the neighborhoods a lot when I was a precinct captain. Now that I'm the ward leader I ain't got the time to do that as much. All of a sudden I'm listening to the stories of every other precinct captain who brings the troubles of their neighbors to me just like my old Chinaman, Chips Delvin, used to have to listen to me. So maybe the committeemen don't get out the vote the same way they used to get out the vote, but no matter what anybody says, the system still works at the grassroots level, and a person without clout can still get some action and satisfaction if he or she knows the right somebody.

I know a lot of somebodies and the ones I don't know my father, Mike, who's a retired fireman and ex–precinct captain hisself, knows.

And the ones Mike don't know Chips Delvin knows.

He's still around at ninety, give or take, sticking his fingers in the pie and his nose in the political business which he turned over to me with his own hands. But that's all right, you can't expect an old fire horse to quit pulling just like that. If you stuck him out to pasture he'd just lay down and die.

I give one night a week to listening to everybody's problems in the storefront office.

I give Saturday afternoons to listening to them what can't make it Monday night over to the back room of Brennan's Tavern where Delvin used to hold his meetings when there was too many people to accommodate in his living room, where I do the same for the sake of tradition. People like some things to change but they also don't like other things to change. The trick is to know which is which.

I used to exercise three nights a week over to the Paradise Health Club while Mary was pregnant. She was eating for two and I was eating for three. Now that she's thin again I don't eat as much as I did eight, nine months ago but I still need to knock off more than a couple of pounds because I ain't walking the neighborhoods as much as I used to for the reasons I already mentioned.

That's the way it goes. There comes a time when you change one little thing in your lifestyle and everything starts falling apart.

So, even though I don't go three times a week I go jump around twice a week, Saturday night and Wednesday night.

Sundays we usually go over to my father and mother-in-law's—who's also my stepmother since she's my father's wife as well as being my wife's mother—for Sunday dinner, my old man suddenly getting very traditional in his old age, even though he jogs five miles a day and is in much better shape than I am.

What I'm trying to point out here is the amount of time I don't get to spend alone with Mary.

So when she talks me into going over to the University of Chicago down across the river to take a couple of night classes, I'm beginning to wonder if the blush is off the romance as they say. I understand that she thinks it'll do my career some good if I brush up on my English grammar and maybe take a course in political science but still and all it bothers me a little. I'm not even sure what she's got in mind for me— most women, I think, dream bigger dreams for their men than their men dream for themselves—but I don't argue about it.

So it's Monday nights and Saturday afternoons—not to mention this special meeting and that special meeting—doing politics, and Tuesday and Saturday nights over to the gym. Sundays with our folks. Wednesday it's English grammar and composition. Thursday it's political science.

Friday nights Mary, who couldn't give up nursing altogether even if she wanted to, unofficially volunteers her time to a family planning and prenatal clinic.

I say unofficially because ever since the federal agency in charge of funding puts out the regulation that money would be taken away if counselors, doctors and nurses in any federally funded clinic mentioned abortion as an alternative to having a child, Mary sits at a desk in the corridor as though she has absolutely nothing to do with the clinic and gives these poor women the information they deserve to have. There's absolutely no paper trail linking her to the clinic and she even pays ten dollars a week rent for the corridor space. So that's the way honest citizens got to split hairs and play games to do what they know is right.

I'm not taking a position for abortion or against abortion. What I'm talking about is a First Amendment right to give and get information vital to a person making a decision about their health and future well-being.

One of the things that gets me is that a lot of the people who are out there protesting in front of the abortion clinics are the same people who bitch and moan about entitlement programs to dependent children and single parents and are also the ones who say build more prisons and expand the death penalty to take care of all the criminals that poverty and social neglect produce.

Anyway, all these obligations don't leave us much time for ourselves. We snatch an hour here and there, now and then.

I got to admit, Mary makes those hours very special.

3

There's maybe twenty of us in the English class. Some are immigrants who already took English as a second language but are still having a little trouble, saying funny things without knowing that they're funny. There's also a couple of dumbos like myself who lived in Chicago all our lives and still say funny things. There's also a big beefy Irishman with sad eyes who is no stranger to me.

Jake O'Meara's an ex-cop—a detective three—who lost his badge and his pension over drink and a woman. After he turned in his badge and gun he hit the skids and was on the long slide to the drunk ward and the grave when he interrupts a robbery in progress in a candy store over in Bridgeport, the neighborhood where Hizzoner was born and raised.

You know how they're all the time saying how you can take the man out of something but you can't take the something out of the man? Well there was enough cop left in O'Meara, or maybe enough despair and shame in his heart, for him to walk into the gun the thief had in his fist. He took three in the belly, but he got the thief and he survived the bullets.

I heard tell it cleaned him up, but it didn't get his badge back and it didn't get him a pension. It got him a citizen's citation, which is something, but not a hell of a lot when you think about it. It also got him the gratitude of the rich old woman who owned and ran the candy store.

That's what I've been told but I don't know the details of how come a rich old woman was working in a neighborhood candy store in Bridgeport, even if she owned it or what, if anything, she did or was doing for O'Meara for his act of heroism.

So when I see O'Meara, I figure I'll not only learn a little something about how to diagram a sentence or whatever it is they do to sentences in grammar classes, but I'd get to hear a pretty good story from O'Meara too.

The instructor's a very pretty young woman with black hair and blue eyes who says right off, "My name's Miss Esper. I don't want to be called Ms. because I'm putting out the word that I'm an unmarried lady. What's wrong with a little subtle advertisement? In fact don't even call me Miss Esper, call me Cora. Esper is Norwegian. I suppose you thought all Scandinavians had blond hair. Well, a lot of Norwegians have black hair like me. I'm going to call the roll."

She goes ahead and calls the roll. We got Bohemians, Germans, Hispanics, Italians, Polish and Irish. We got a couple of blacks, one with an Irish name and one with a Polish name.

When she calls O'Meara's name and he answers, she looks up as though she's getting a look at somebody she's heard about or might like to know.

When she calls my name, she looks up and smiles at me.

"I know we've got a lot of people in this class who are very new to the English language and some who may not be new to it but are not too comfortable with the grammar. There's an odd thing about how people use language. Very often we speak it differently than we write it. A lot of us have very large reading vocabularies and comparatively small speaking vocabularies."

She lays a little tape recorder on the desk.

"I'm going to ask each one of you to get up and talk for three minutes." She glances at the wall clock. "That's going to chew up most of the two hours. So, who wants to start?"

Nobody volunteers.

I've never been shy about speaking up but nobody wants to be pushy right off the bat with a bunch of people who might get the idea you're a know-it-all. Also, nobody wants to be teacher's pet even if the teacher's as good-looking as Cora.

"Mr. Flannery," she says, "how about you? I never thought politicians were shy."

I get on my feet and I says, "Well, I ain't exactly a politician. I'm a citizen who's interested in government and I figure government is every citizen's business."

She's holding up a finger and fiddling with the recorder.

"Would you mind starting again?" she says.

"Well, I ain't really started," I says. "I was just sort of answering your remark. What would you like me to talk about?"

"If you'd like me to choose a theme, why don't I choose a theme for everyone? How about three minutes on who you are, what you do for a living and a little something about your family?"

"Okay," I says. "My name's Jimmy Flannery and I work for Streets and Sanitation in the Department of Sewers. I'm also the committeeman for the Democratic party in the Twenty-seventh Ward. I'm married and we just had a baby. Kathleen's six months old. Listening to myself tell it, I realize that I got those three important things in my life the wrong way around in the order of importance. My family comes first, my work for the Party comes second and my work in the sewers comes third. But you look at it another way and they're all part of the same situation. Right this minute I couldn't imagine my life with any one of them missing. I mean I could do without the sewers but I couldn't do without the paycheck."

That gets a big laugh.

"It wasn't so long ago I was a precinct captain who inspected the sewers when they had to be inspected and used to go over to Dan Blatna's Sold Out saloon over in the Thirty-second on the Northwest Side to have some kielbasa and cabbage with my old man every Wednesday night. But now that I'm married with a baby we don't do that anymore. Besides which my old man just got married—remarried—after all these years my mother's been gone . . . God rest her soul."

I notice that Cora's grinning at me and it knocks me off my pace a little bit.

"Am I doing or saying something funny I don't know I'm doing or saying?" I asks.

"I'm sorry, Mr. Flannery," Cora says. "It's only that I was thinking while you were talking that I'd be ready to vote for you if there were an election tomorrow morning. For a man who's not a politician, you certainly have all the moves."

That gets another laugh, which I don't mind, because you get people laughing with you and you get people liking you, and I'd rather have people liking me than not.

"Anyway, here I am a committeeman for the Twenty-seventh," I says, "with a family and a future. My wife says it wouldn't do me any harm if I learned to talk a little better and write a little better, though she admits that most of what I read I understand pretty good. Just like you say, Miss Esper—Cora—I know more words than I use in ordinary conversation. Also I'm taking another class in political science tomorrow night, so maybe I'll finally learn something about what I been doing half my life."

"Which is what they call the bottom line, isn't it, Mr. Flannery—Jimmy? I mean to say that everybody in this room has been successful in their lives. A lot of you had the courage to emigrate to a new country where the language was unknown to you and here you are trying to improve your skills all the time. So, I want you to understand, I'm not saying that learning to write and speak according to a set of standard rules will make you a better person. All it will do is enable you to make yourself better understood in a greater number of situations."

She thanks me then and asks who'd like to be next. Some hands go up.

It goes on like that until we're down to the last half dozen, which there are no volunteers among them. O'Meara is one of the holdouts.

So now she has to pick them out and she picks O'Meara.

He gets to his feet and just stands there for maybe a whole minute.

"Mister . . . ?" she says.

"O'Meara," he says. "Jake O'Meara."

"Well, Jake, that's a start," she says very softly. "What do you do for a living? If you don't mind telling us."

A grin like a twist of pain pulls up the corners of his mouth, but it's gone before you can really get a good look at it, and he says, "I take care of a dog."

"You're a veterinary or a groomer?"

"No, I take care of one dog. I just take this one dog for walks and see that he's fed. I live in the house with this one dog."

"Oh?" she says, looking puzzled, looking a little pained, as though she understands that he's opening up something here which could be embarrassing for him, but she don't know exactly how. "Is this a special dog?"

"I'd say he was very special dog. He's the dog what keeps a roof over my head and food on my plate and whiskey in my glass."

"Are you caring for a champion? Are you a trainer or

a handler?" she asks, like she knows she shouldn't be asking any questions but can't help herself, like a doctor who's probing around trying to find out where it hurts but is afraid of touching the spot where it hurts so bad that the patient will scream or pass out.

"Well, I did this favor for somebody," he says, like he's desperate, "this old woman who had a lot of money. Had this old mansion in Bridgeport. She's got this dog, this old dog, must be thirteen, even fourteen. She had the dog since it was a pup and she was worried about what her relatives would do with the dog—to the dog—when she died. She was old and she knew she was going to die pretty soon and she was worried that her nieces and nephews would put the dog down. They couldn't put her down because she was old but they could put the dog down. We do that, you know? We won't let some person who's suffering the agonies of hell get help leaving this life, but we'll put down a dog or a cat or a horse just because we've got no use for them anymore."

"Mr. O'Meara. Jake," Cora says, like she's afraid he's going to start crying, and then she'll start crying.

But now that she's got him started he can't stop.

"But the old lady's no fool. She and her husband had scrimped and saved and made themselves a lot of money in the futures market just with the savings they managed to drag out of a neighborhood candy store and added properties to it—like the old mansion—but they held on to the old candy store they started with and the old lady—Mrs. Papadopolous, she was Greek—still worked there up till the time she died. That's when her relatives find out that she's determined to take care of that old dog. It's in her will that the dog is to live in the house until it dies. All the rest of her property, the money and stocks and everything, she's got put into a trust so the interest will pay for the gas and electric, the taxes and things like that. And she makes it that I'm the caretaker for the dog. For Billy. That's the dog's name. I got a job and an income as long as that dog's alive. So that's what I do," he ends up, and sits down.

You don't have to be a psychologist or anything like that to know that he's ashamed that he's making his living, such as it is, watching out for an old dog.

Then he pops up again. "Thank you," he says.

And you don't have to be a genius to figure out that he was glad of the chance to spill his guts hoping he'd feel better about it.

"Thank you, Jake," Cora says, and right there, from the look in her eye, I know she's got an interest in O'Meara which has got nothing to do with how he speaks English.

4

I know the teacher of political science we got on
Thursday nights. I met him once or twice before, but I
didn't think he'd remember me.

His name is Frank Vollmer and he's a partner in the
law firm of Crank, Edgar, Asher, Somebody and Somebody which I remember because they do a lot of business with the city.

He's a tall, slim guy about forty-five, forty-six,
with a very impressive way about him as he stands
there at the front of the room, reading a letter and
smiling as the new class comes straggling in, giving
one another the old one eye, trying to figure out why
this one or that one is coming to a class in politics and
government.

The people in my English class are there for reasons
that are probably a lot more obvious than the ones taking political science. There's some youngsters who are
probably picking up the slack in their programs, either making up failed classes or earning extra credits.

There's a couple of scholarly types and a couple who look like neighborhood activists who want to get the straight theory behind what they been doing all this time, just like me. The rest are just filling in the lonely nights with something they figure might be interesting.

Every student in the room could give a pretty good reason why they're giving up Thursday night. What I can't figure out is what a person like Frank Vollmer is doing up there at the front of the room in his hundred-dollar shirt, two-hundred-dollar pants, four-hundred-dollar shoes, and five-hundred-dollar sweater.

When I was parking my beat-up Chevy in the lot, I see him just locking up a twelve-cylinder XJ6 Jaguar with a metallic silver-gray paint job.

I mean what is a power hitter like Vollmer doing giving up one night a week to stand up in front of twenty people? I understand that there are some people who like to teach and some who think they owe something to society and want to give something back, but I don't think Vollmer's one of them.

Besides his practice with the law firm, he's also the chairman of the Municipal Pier, Canal, Garages, Public Curbs and Expansion Agency, which gives him control over most of the city contracts for public construction and the legal and insurance contracts that serve the public construction industry.

Here's a cloutmeister what charges four hundred dollars an hour, who probably ain't had his shoes shined while they was on his feet for twenty years because he'd be losing too much money just standing there while his slip-ons were getting buffed, giving up

three hours, seven to ten, every Thursday night for at
least thirteen weeks.

It's nothing I got to worry about, but you'll excuse
me if I'm a little suspicious about this man's motives.

He folds the letter three times and tucks it into a
wallet which he takes from his back pocket, clears his
throat, looks us over like we was some alien creatures
he's got to identify and describe to hisself before he can
go on and says, "My name's Vollmer. I'm an attorney.
Here's the way I'd like to work it. Every time you get
up to speak, state your name first. That way, after a
couple of sessions, I'll know most of you. I know a
couple of you already. I see Vince Pastorelli over there.
Glad to see you, Vince. And over there I see the pride
of the Twenty-seventh, their new warlord—committeeman—Jimmy Flannery."

He gives Vince and me a couple of nods and a raised
hand like we was fighters in the audience at the Friday
nights and he was the ring announcer. I start wondering if Vollmer's ready to run for public office. How
bad could it look on his credentials if he could say he
taught political science to a group of the underprivileged? Underprivileged compared to him, that is.

"Would you mind telling us, Vince, why you're taking this class?"

This Pastorelli, who I don't know but who I've
heard about in connection with Carmine DiBella, the
godfather of the most powerful of the Chicago Fami-
lies, gets to his feet. He's maybe fifty-five or sixty, a
lumbering giant with the bashful appearance of inno-
cence some bone-breakers I know got. The kind that is
. . . are . . . very dumb and very, very loyal. But I

learned a long time ago not to judge a book by its cover, like they say.

I knew a priest once, Father Patrick Herlihy, when he wasn't dressed in his collar, wearing a pair of slacks and a sports jacket, he looked like a hustler and a pimp. He had that good-looking, easy way about him which made the ladies eye him up more than once, more than twice. The strain got so bad, what with girls and women from the parish hitting on him, that he joined a monastery. Later on, I heard tell, he was made the confessor for the sisters of a cloistered convent, which, the way old Father Mulhaney tells it, was not so much like putting the fox in with the chickens as putting the rooster in with the vixens. I've always found that priests are a lot more honest about the power of sex than the average layman. Father Mulhaney knew from what he spoke, because the next thing I heard was that Father Herlihy had finally succumbed to temptation. He'd left the monastery and the priesthood and married Sister Clothilde Kranowski who, naturally, left her order as well.

Pastorelli stands there grinning foolishly, looking very confused. Finally he says, "I was told to come by my boss, Mr. D."

"That's good. That's good," Vollmer says, smiling on Pastorelli in this benevolent way, waiting to hear more, but there ain't any more. Pastorelli just stands there looking foolish until Vollmer tells him to sit down. Then he turns to me and says, "How about you, Jimmy?"

While I'm getting to my feet I notice that Vollmer's frowning a little bit as he keeps looking at Pastorelli as though he's wondering—just like I'm wondering—if the big man's as dumb as he seems.

"I'm here for the same reason Mr. Pastorelli's here," I says. "My boss told me to come. My boss being my wife, Mary, who had a baby six months ago which, for reasons I ain't been able to figure out yet, convinces her that I should come back to school and finish my education."

I get a couple of laughs with my little speech, during which Pastorelli sits down, looking both puzzled and relieved.

"All right," Vollmer says. "I see no reason why we shouldn't start right in with a little talk on the historical forms of government starting with tribal and clan chieftains and leading to constitutional monarchs and democratic presidents."

I notice that Pastorelli is already looking sleepy.

"In the beginning there was the territorial imperative," Vollmer says.

5

It used to be that my old man was over to our place half the time, sitting down to supper and watching television with us in the living room afterwards. But ever since he got married to Mary's mother, Charlotte, and he moved into her house—where she used to live with her sister, Aunt Sada—over to Mount Prospect, we don't see him much anymore except on Sundays when we go to them.

Aunt Sada insisted on moving out. She got herself a little flat over in the Fifth Ward, in a neighborhood which was heavily Jewish years ago, went black, and is going Jewish again.

She comes over for Sunday dinner too, her and my old man arguing politics while Charlotte and Mary prepare the meal and I sit there, with Kathleen on my lap, taking it all in.

So this Sunday Mike asks me how things are going at school and I tell him it's too early to know anything since I've only been going for three weeks and I'm still

saying "ain't" and I still don't quite know the difference between a duchy and a principality.

"Well, that's easy," Mike says. "The duchy's run by a
duke and the principality's run by a prince."

"That much I figured out," I says. "What I don't
know is where they stand in the pecking order. Who
they got to go to for permission to do this or that.
What they got to give to the overboss and what they
can expect in return. Speaking of which."

"Which what?"

"Bosses, under and over. You happen to know a big
Italian by the name of Pastorelli?"

"He used to run errands for Carmine DiBella last I
heard about him. He's a small potato, a goofus. Not
even a foot soldier."

"You happen to know if the DiBellas got anything
to do with Frank Vollmer?"

"The Mob's into construction, they're into concrete,
they're into trash removal. Frank Vollmer gives out
contracts. How could there not be a connection?"
Aunt Sada says.

"Is it true that Carmine retired this year?" I asks.

"He did. He went back to Sicily. He's got a villa
overlooking a town there. He owns the town," Mike
says.

"So who took over for him?"

"Nobody knows for sure. It could be his sister's son.
It could be his nephew, the son of his oldest brother
who died several years ago and never had much to do
with the family business. It could be his youngest
brother."

"The only brother still alive," Aunt Sada chimes in.

"I was going to say. The way I understand it there's a power struggle going on but this time it looks like they agreed there'd be no going to the mattresses, no gunfights in the restaurants, nobody gunned down in a barbershop while he's getting a shave."

"So what qualifications for the top job are they putting on the table?" I asks.

Mike shrugs his shoulders and Aunt Sada shows me the upraised palms of her hands, both of them asking the same question, Who's to say?

"So why are you asking?" Aunt Sada asks.

"A bent nose by the name of Pastorelli in my political science class says he works for a Mr. D. So I naturally wondered."

"On the basis of an initial letter, you're leaping to the conclusion that this Pastorelli works for a gangster by the name of DiBella and is, therefore, a gangster himself?" Aunt Sada said.

"It catches my attention that he falls asleep in class as soon as he gets there and that makes me wonder why he's taking a class in adult education in the first place."

"Maybe the man aspires to better things but puts in such long hours on his job that he just can't manage to stay awake."

"If he's putting in long hours it's breaking legs and busting heads," Mike says.

"The man's Italian and falls asleep in class which makes him not only dumb but a thug?" Aunt Sada says.

"Nobody said he was dumb."

"Jimmy said he had a bent nose and in your jargon that means the man is dumb."

"In what jargon?" Mike asks.

"The way you Irish talk," Aunt Sada says, sticking her foot right in it up to the hip.

It used to be that half the time I said something Mike would jump on me and then turn it around so it looked like I said what he really said and vice versa. Now that he's got Aunt Sada to disagree with it sort of gets me off the hook.

"Aha," he says, "here you are accusing my son of jumping to conclusions based on ethnic prejudice and you just done the same thing making cracks about the Irish."

"Speaking of which," I says.

"Speaking of what?" they both say together.

"You happen to remember a cop by the name of Jake O'Meara?"

"Pothole?" Mike says.

"Who what?"

"Pothole O'Meara," Mike says.

"Why did they call him Pothole?" Aunt Sada asks.

"I don't know. That's something lost in the mists of time. But that's what they called him. Made detective. Got three or four citations for bravery. Lost it all."

"Drink and women," I says.

"The women came first. Two women. His wife and his girlfriend."

"An alley cat," Aunt Sada said.

"Alley *cats*," Mike says. "The wife was by way of being a tramp."

"You know that for a fact?" Sada says, immediately leaping to the woman's defense.

"I didn't hop into bed with her, if that's what you mean, Sada, but I knew more than one who did," Mike says.

"Firemen?" she says, like that said it all.

"And other cops. Men he worked with. That was the worst. That's what drove Pothole crazy."

"So what happened?" Sada asks.

"What happened was she ran off with the mailman."

Sada laughed and I started to grin, like he just told one of those old jokes about the mailman and the housewife.

"I mean it," he says. "She was having it off with the mailman along with everybody else." Then he grins too. "I guess she found real love with the Post Office."

"She liked uniforms," Sada murmurs in a kind of thoughtful way.

"So after that he hit the bottle pretty hard. He'd worked vice now and then and knew a lot of hookers. One of them got his attention. He thought it was true love, lightning striking for a second time. Lucky him. A lot of people think a reformed hooker makes the best wife."

"He married her?" I asks.

"He was getting around to it. They was living to-gether and playing house, but she couldn't handle the nights alone while he was out there making the streets safe. So she went out to the neighborhood bar, just for a little conversation, a little fun. The first thing you know she was turning tricks. He caught her at it and beat the hell out of the john. Could be he was going to kill her. At least that's how the cops found him when they busted in on a neighbor's complaint, Pothole standing over her, threatening her with his service revolver."

"They busted him?"

"They canned him. He was a loose cannon and a drunk one at that."

"So what about the act of heroism?"

"The old lady in the candy store?"

"Yeah, that one."

"There was some who said he did it because he wanted to get back on the force. A lot more said he wanted the thief to do for him what he couldn't do for himself, but the thief was a lousy shot."

"Who was the old lady?" I asks.

"I don't remember her name."

"Mrs. Papadopolous. O'Meara told us when we introduced ourselves in English class."

"That so? Well, anyway, she had this old house in Bridgeport."

"A mansion, O'Meara says."

"I suppose you could call it that. At least it was a big old house. I wouldn't want to live in it even if it was for free. I understand that's the deal he made with the old lady before she died. He'd live in the old house and take care of her dog—"

"Billy," I says.

"—until it died."

"What the hell," Mike says. "Why are you asking me? You seem to know more about it than I do."

"Well, I was hoping you had a couple of facts I didn't have."

"One fact you maybe don't know is that her relatives did everything they could to break the will so they could get their hands on the old lady's money and property but she figured for that probability and left a lawyer in charge of fighting such claims."

"So they attack the will enough times, the lawyer could end up with all the marbles."

"Ain't it the truth. If the relatives are stubborn enough and dumb enough to keep on trying, it'll be a race to see if the dog dies before the lawyer strips the estate for fees and tosses Pothole and the dog both out into the street."

"Sometimes you can protect yourself against everybody except the people you hire to protect you against the people out to do you an injury," Aunt Sada says.

Me and Mike both say "Amen" to that.

6

It's the eighth week of political science class. Vollmer's giving us one of his fifty-dollar lectures. This one happens to be on the principle of the "town hall as a prime example of participatory democracy and the changes that growing populations brought with them as the cities aggregated into political structures too big to function so that representative government took over more and more, meaning that there was a separation of different political philosophies into parties, which demanded organization from the precincts through the wards and districts. . . . " The idea being to elect candidates to the city council.

Pastorelli's already asleep at his desk at the back of the room, his head thrown back and his mouth open.

Every two minutes Vollmer looks at his watch and starts racing through his notes until, after only five bucks' worth of the fifty-buck lecture, he says, "That's the material for discussion this evening. I've got pressing business which will take me about an hour so I'm going to turn the discussion over to Jim Flannery as the moderator. Flannery knows as much or more about party organization than I do, which means you're probably going to get some war stories that might be both interesting and entertaining." Then he hurries out with a wave of his hand.

I get up to the front of the class, feeling as foolish as I did when I was a kid and was asked to take over a class while the teacher left the room for a minute; like I was being singled out as teacher's pet. It's funny how feelings like that hang on all your life.

"I don't know about war stories though there's been times when campaigns have looked a lot like combat on election day," I says. "I never used them methods getting out the vote. I never tried to intimidate the other side."

"You got a safe Democratic ward," a guy named Jack Brewster pipes up. "The people in your ward can't even read the word Republican."

"It's true this town's been Democratic from back in the days when Hinky Dink Kenna and Bathhouse John Coughlan ran the First," I says, "but the state-house has practically always gone to the Republicans, so it evens out.

"You hear all the colorful stories—the war stories— and you hear all the tall tales and funny jokes about 'vote early and vote often' and voting the names off the tombstones, but what a lot of people don't hear is how much and what kind of work goes into building a grassroots organization."

"It's no secret," Brewster says. "You buy votes with jobs."

"No more. There ain't many patronage jobs around."

"There's always a way. You Democrats always find an angle."

"I didn't know you was a Republican, Jack."

"I ain't. I'm a Reform Independent."

"Well, you had a good shot with a good man," I says. "But it looks like you couldn't keep it together. You lost it. And you know why? The Regular Democratic Organization had an organization ready to stand up again and your bunch had no organization at all. After your man dropped dead with his heart attack—may he rest in peace—you were so busy fighting over who was going to take his place, you couldn't come up with a candidate that was good enough."

Brewster moves his elbow like he's brushing off my remarks and knocks a textbook off his desk. It hits the floor like a gunshot and wakes up Pastorelli, who closes his mouth, blinks, looks all around in a vague way, sees that it's me not Vollmer standing up in front of the class and rushes on out.

"Well, Jack, it looks like we chased one student out of the room."

"At least we woke him up," Brewster says, getting back his good nature.

We go on talking about how machine politics worked in the big cities of America until Vollmer comes back about an hour later than the hour he said he'd be gone.

He's brushed and combed, like he usually is, but he also looks a little frayed around the edges, like he's been pulled through a knothole, as my father would say. He's paler than he should be and it's pretty clear that his mind is elsewhere. He takes over the class and we rattle around for another five minutes. There's only ten minutes left anyway, so he finally just thanks everybody for coming like he does at the end of every session and tells us to be careful going home. Then he asks me to wait a minute.

When the room's empty he comes over and sits down at the desk next to mine.

"I just wanted to tell you how well I think you're doing in this class," he says.

"That's very gratifying," I says.

"You ever think of going for a degree?"

"A degree in what?"

"Well, a degree in law, for instance."

"I'll have to take a pass on that, Counselor," I says. "From what I read this country's already lawyered to death. They're graduating thousands every year. You get all those people out there with all that training and all them—those—degrees in their hot little hands, and they got a natural itch to do something with all that education. If there ain't enough work for everybody, lawyering's one of the few professions I can think of where they can go out and make a job for themselves."

He stands up. "Some do that, I'll admit," he says, "but there are doctors who perform unnecessary operations every day of the week. Let's go; walk me out."

"Just my point," I says, standing up myself and joining him as he strolls out the door. "I didn't say lawyers was the only ones. And I'm not saying that these doctors you're mentioning haven't convinced themselves that this patient needs a hysterectomy and that patient needs a bypass. There ain't a lot of evil people deliberating cutting people up, I'm just saying when the decision's got to be made, five or ten thousand dollars can make the difference in the final decision."

"You're not saying you want fewer doctors because some abuse their position?"

"I'd have to think about that," I says. "But ask me the same question about lawyers and I'd have to say fewer would be better. I see it in my ward. It used to be that people came to the precinct captains, to the rabbis or the priests, to their family doctors maybe or some attorney what had an office over the drugstore and got advice practically off the cuff. Arguments and quarrels was settled between neighbors that way. Now if they don't hear from me what they want to hear they go out and sue. Spend a lot of money for very little satisfaction."

"A career in the law can lead to other things nowadays."

"Well, there's that. Real estate, the boards of corporations, and politics seem to be soaking up a lot of the excess lawyers. I can understand that. When it pays you to understand the rules so you can bend them, some people would say you were a fool not to study up. But you see what I do in the ward, I don't do for money. Maybe I don't even do it for my neighbors . . . what you'd call my constituency. Maybe I do it for myself because I been brought up to feel good about helping somebody else."

"Perhaps you should've been a priest," Vollmer says.

"That thought never entered my mind. I ain't a professional do-gooder."

"What are you, then?"

"More like a professional busybody. I'm one of them people other people tell to butt out except when the sidewalk's caving in or the roof's coming down around their heads. I like being a busybody. I might even start a club."

By this time we're in the parking lot. We get to my car first.

He points and says, "My car's over there." Then he says good night and walks away.

I watch him passing through the shadows and the pools of lights from the streetlights. I got this uneasy feeling that he didn't want to talk to me about how good I was doing in class and how I should maybe go on with an education and maybe become a lawyer. He wanted to talk to me about something else and then changed his mind at the last minute. I got no idea what he wanted to talk about. I'm pretty good about knowing when somebody wants to confide in me, but I can't read minds.

I get in my Chevy and have the usual trouble getting the engine to turn over. While I'm pumping the pedal, he drives by in his Jaguar. I look over as he leaves the parking lot and turns right toward the main boulevard. I notice that the Jag looks a different color under the lights, and then my engine kicks over and I'm busy nursing it into life.

7

I go visit my old Chinaman, Chips Delvin, on the average of once a week, no particular time or day, just stopping by when I got a spare hour. This Monday morning I got a reason, a couple of questions. Just this morning, going through the obits (they say that priests, undertakers, the very old and politicians are the most faithful readers of the obits), I see that one Vincent Pastorelli was being buried out of Collisimo's Funeral Home. There's no details about how or exactly when he passed away. When I ring the doorbell at Delvin's Mrs. Thimble, his housekeeper, opens the door and says, "He told me to tell you he's not at home."

"You mean he's otherwise occupied?" I says.

"Not at home."

"You mean he's got visitors?"

"Not at home is what he said and that's what I'm telling you," she says.

"Well, wait a minute," I says, "I just saw the curtains twitch as I was walking up the steps, so I know he's not taking a nap, he's just sitting there looking out like he does when he's got nothing else to do."

"I got plenty to do, plenty to do," Delvin shouts from inside the living room.

"I just stopped by to say hello," I shout back.

"Did you say something, Mrs. Thimble?" he asks in this sweet la-de-dah voice.

She closes her eyes in a long-suffering way, and I can tell he's been acting like a child again over something or other.

"It's me, Jimmy Flannery," I yell.

"Is there someone at the door, Mrs. Thimble?" he asks.

Mrs. Thimble sighs and rolls her eyes.

"It's Mr. Flannery," she says.

"Oh, is that so," he says, like he finally hears her but couldn't hear me. "Ain't that nice? Well, show him in. Show him in."

I step into the hall with the old-time pictures of family and friends fading into sepia memories on the wall.

"Would you like a refreshment, Mr. Flannery?" Mrs. Thimble asks in a very polite way, which is unusual for her, she being generally grumpier and harder to get along with than Delvin himself. I think he's been so bad today that she's cozying up to me as the nearest friend she can call on if he gets any worse.

"And a small refreshment for the host, Mrs. Thimble," Delvin says.

"The doctor says not," she whispers.

"Well, doctors have been saying not for the last

forty years and he's buried six of them," I whisper back.

She gives me a quick grin of surrender, a comment on the vagaries of fate.

I go into the living room. There's sheer ecru curtains and old cream-colored lace curtains at the windows down to the floor. Old Turkey carpets piled one on top of the other. Big overstuffed chairs with lace doilies protecting the backs and arms. A room out of the turn of the century smelling of dust.

Delvin's sitting in the big chair by the window. The floor lamp at his elbow is on. He's sitting under the pool of yellow light blinking at me like some old walrus on a rock, a spray of hair across his freckled dome, a mustache like a small hedge what needs clipping under this nose like a baby's fist.

"Why did you tell Mrs. Thimble that you wasn't at home?"

"I didn't know who it was until you declared yourself," he says.

"You saw it was me coming up the block."

"Well, I'm a busy man. People can't just drop in whenever they feel like it."

"I been dropping in whenever I needed to see you since I was a kid."

He brightens up. "You're here for a consultation?" I get it now. He's got all the time in the world for me if I'm there to ask a favor but if I'm there doing a duty dance, visiting an old friend who's out of the loop— like they say in Washington—then he don't want to take the charity.

"A little information."

"Take a load off your feet," he says, adjusting himself in his chair, ready for a conversation, ready to deliver me a judgment from on high.

Mrs. Thimble comes in with a tray on which there's two glasses with a finger of whiskey in each one, a split of ginger ale and a small bowl of ice cubes.

I don't drink and practically everybody knows it. Every time I get served a drink in Delvin's house, he snatches it out of my hand quicker than a wink and pretends he didn't. Mrs. Thimble's standing there.

"What are you doing, woman," Delvin asks, "waiting for a tip?"

She huffs and leaves the room.

Delvin pours my finger of whiskey into his glass and pops in one ice cube. Then he puts a half a dozen cubes in my glass and pours me the ginger ale.

"No thanks," I says.

"You better drink up or you'll insult Mrs. Thimble."

"She ain't fooled," I says. "She knows I don't drink and that you drink my drinks."

"Don't you think I know that?" he says. "What kind of a damn fool do you take me for?"

"Then why do you bother pretending?"

"You ain't learned a hellofalot about people, have you, Flannery? Look. You tell a lie or practice a deceit. This other person knows that you're telling a lie or practicing a deceit. How are they ever going to catch you at it again? How are they going to reinforce their opinion of you as a cheat and a liar, thereby reconfirming their own moral superiority, if they come right out and say they caught you? I mean you can feel smug about knowing something you think the other person don't know you know, but you can't use it against them unless you're ready to end the game."

What he says gets my wheels turning. I can't help feeling—like I been feeling right from the moment I laid eyes on Pastorelli—that he was playing some kind of game with Vollmer, him sitting there week after week fast asleep while Vollmer lectures, until that one night when Vollmer leaves the class to me and takes a walk with Pastorelli leaving right after.

A memory's coming back to me but before I can get a clear view of the picture that's starting to form, Delvin knocks it out of my head rattling on about how he hears tell they're closing down Schaller's Pump across the street from Democratic party headquarters. I ain't got the heart to tell him it's still open even if he can't get there.

Finally I get around to asking what I came to ask.

"You know a Vincent Pastorelli?" I says.

"Sure, he used to hang around with Carmine Di-Bella."

"As a bodyguard or a what?"

"An old friend from their boyhood days together in Little Italy. Actually Carmine was maybe ten, fifteen years older than Vincent. He took him under his wing because Vinnie was none too bright. He was no body-guard. Pastorelli wasn't quick enough to guard a mouse. He wasn't quick enough to get out of the way of whatever killed him. He's dead, you know?"

"That's why I'm asking. He was in this night school class with me. He leaves in the middle of the class last

Thursday night and here it is Monday and he's getting buried."

"What kind of class you taking with Pastorelli?" Delvin asks.

"Political science," I says.

"What do you want to study that stuff for? It'll only confuse you. The only science you got to know is to do favors and get paid back favors. But the question that comes to mind is what the hell was Pastorelli doing taking any kind of class at all? He could hardly write his own name."

"I had the feeling that he was there to keep an eye on somebody."

"Who?"

"Frank Vollmer."

"The attorney?"

"That's right. He teaches the class."

"I wonder why Pastorelli would be keeping an eye on Vollmer. What could be the connection?"

"You took the words right out of my mouth."

Delvin thinks a minute.

"You want a piece of advice?"

"That's why I'm here drinking your ginger ale while you're drinking my whiskey," I says.

"In which you don't indulge," Delvin says. "My advice is, keep your nose out of it."

"I thought I'd just go over to the funeral parlor and pay my respects. After all, Pastorelli and me was classmates."

"Send a card. There's a power struggle going on in the DiBella family. Maybe that's what killed Pastorelli. You don't want to be an unfortunate innocent bystander and the best way to avoid that is to stay out of the DiBella parish."

I finish my ginger ale and put the empty glass down on the tray. I stand up ready to go.

"You ain't going to take my advice, are you?" Delvin says.

"I'm going to think about it. One more thing. With Carmine DiBella retired to Sicily, you happen to know where he's put his loyalty? Is he with one of the nephews or the brother?"

"That'd be Anthony, Bruno and Joseph, right?"

"If you say so. I don't know the gentlemen."

"Well, I don't know which one of them would give Pastorelli a job, as useless as he was. My bet would be that if Pastorelli didn't go with Carmine—if he wanted to stay here in the States—Carmine would've asked his brother, Joseph, to give him a job. Keep him occupied."

"Thanks," I says.

"So you're going to have a talk with Joseph Di-Bella," Delvin says.

"It's only a maybe," I says.

"You know, Jimmy," Delvin says, "I'm ninety years old but I got a feeling I'll be going to your funeral before you go to mine."

8

I go over to the funeral home where Pastorelli is laid out for anybody what wants to take a look.

There's maybe fifty, sixty people in the slumber room, sitting around on folding chairs except for three men and three women who're sitting in fake Louis the something upholstered armchairs with these skinny gilt legs and lavender velvet seats and backs.

Practically every person, man or woman, is wearing black, some Italians like a lot of the Irish being very attached to the old ways.

When I take off my hat it's like every eyeball in the room comes my way, redheads not being the most common thing among the Sicilians. So they spot me for an outsider right off the bat.

A little man wearing a black three-piece suit, which he manages to make look like striped pants and a cutaway, comes tiptoeing over to me with the oily assurance of the high-priced spread. I get the picture right away. In the absence of any next of kin or even a best friend to claim the duty and privilege, somebody's decided to let the funeral home director do the honors of checking out any doubtful visitors.

"Can I say?" he whispers into my ear.

His breath smells of them little licorice bits that some people suck to hide an odor.

"My name's Jimmy Flannery," I says in a murmur.

"You were a friend of Mr. Pastorelli's?"

"More like an acquaintance," I says.

That don't create a lot of interest. He looks more than a little disapproving like I was one of them curiosity seekers who like to go around viewing corpses.

"I was in Vincent's class over to the University," I says.

He smiles at that. After all, two people pursuing an education together creates a bond that might not make them old pals but surely more than strangers. He holds up a finger and goes toddling off to whisper into the ear of the oldest of the three men sitting in the good chairs, who have not taken their eyes off me since I walked in and took off my hat.

I don't have to be a genius to figure out that the man the undertaker's reporting to is Joseph DiBella, Carmine's younger brother. His lips twitch. He puts this grave smile on his face and beckons me over with a crooked finger as the messenger trots away.

I noticed many times before that when a stranger attends a funeral—once some bona fides is established—they get treated with special consideration. I think it's because friends and family—no matter who they might be—are touched by the concern of somebody unknown to them, curious about this example of a life the dear departed lived which they knew nothing about and pleased that this person is taking the time to pay his or her respects.

As I walk the thirty feet to the chairs closest to the coffin, I'm guessing that the younger man, with the kind of beard he's got to shave at least twice a day, sitting on Joseph's left is Anthony, Carmine DiBella's late brother's son and the other one, on the right, who is thinner and more refined looking is the nephew, Bruno, the son of Carmine's sister, Rose Falduto. You can see I asked around and got some more information. But I didn't get around to getting more information about the ladies.

The middle-aged woman wearing the comfortable shoes sitting next to Joseph is clearly his wife.

I don't know if the pretty blonde with the brown eyes and bee-stung lips sitting next to Anthony is his wife or girlfriend. Likewise for the black-haired woman sitting next to Bruno—who could even be a sister. Whatever she is, she's got a nice figure even though she's buttoned up practically to the chin. She's also wearing a long skirt which covers up a lot more of her legs than does the blonde's who tugs at the hem of her skirt as I bend over to shake Joseph's hand just to let me know she's got very attractive thighs.

"My name's Jimmy Flannery," I says. "Vincent and me was taking a class—"

"I know. Mr. Collisimo just told us. Was you good friends?"

"Well, I can't exactly say that. I mean we only went to eight, maybe nine classes before . . . "

"Sure, sure." He looks right, then left. "Maybe one of you could get a chair?" he says.

"That's okay," I says. "I'll just go say a little prayer."

He puts his hand on my sleeve. "But you come back here and sit with me when you're through."

I go over and kneel on the prayer stool and fold my hands. I got to admit I ain't very religious anymore—I won't go into why not—but if I go into a mosque, I take off my shoes, or into a shul, I wear a yarmulke, or into a Catholic church I genuflect in front of the altar. Simple respect for the way other people think. Also I say a few kind words for the dead, putting aside the fact that I might not altogether believe that there's a God up there watching out for every sparrow that falls. It's the kind thought for one person to another I'm talking about.

Vincent Pastorelli's laying there and I got to admit that he don't look too much different than he looked most of the time in class. Because he was always sleeping then and he looks like he's sleeping now. I notice there's some bruising on his neck and jaw which the cosmetics ain't entirely covering up. So, I wonder what that could be all about.

When I get to my feet and turn around, I see that the older woman's left the chair she was sitting in vacant and Joseph DiBella's calling me over with that crooked finger again.

I sit down next to him and says, "I hope I didn't make your wife give up her seat."

"My wife? Oh, that ain't my wife. That's my sister. My wife's sitting over there."

I look where he's pointing and I see three old

women dressed in black and a young woman also dressed in black but looking like she's going to a cocktail party, sitting all together having a talk. I don't know which one of the older women is Joseph DiBella's wife and I don't ask. The younger woman stands up and looks my way. She's got the kind of body what looks naked even when she's fully dressed. She'd look naked wearing a mackinaw.

"You know the rest of the family?" Joseph DiBella goes on.

"I don't think I've had the pleasure," I says.

He reaches across me and taps the guy with the heavy beard who ain't paying anybody any attention on the arm. I can see he's trying to figure out an excuse to get out of there just like his uncle's wife was able to do. "This is my nephew, Anthony DiBella," Joseph says. "This is Jimmy Cannery."

"Flannery," I says, correcting him and reaching out to shake Anthony's tough but flaccid paw.

"Hey, Flannery. I'm sorry," Joseph says.

"That's all right," I says.

"Flannery," he says again, like the name's finally coming through. "You knew my brother," Joseph says.

"We met once or twice."

"I remember now. You walked in on a party my brother was at over to Poppsie Hanneman's—"

"Poppsie and me are old friends," I says, hoping he won't remember the details of the time I insulted Carmine DiBella to his face because I couldn't figure out any other way to protect myself.

"He liked to tell the story how this cocky little Irishman tells him to lay off or else right in front of—"

"I was maybe a little rash in them days," I says.

"—a room full of people. He used to get a big laugh out of it, how this little Irishman wasn't afraid to do what ninety-nine percent—a hundred percent—of the hard guys were afraid to do. You remember the story your uncle used to tell, Anthony?" Joseph asks, laughing in this soft way, really enjoying it.

"I remember," Anthony says, giving me this look as though he's telling me that even though his old man didn't want to step on me and get the bottom of his shoe dirty, he wouldn't mind squashing me if I give him the least cause.

Meanwhile, the blonde, who is introduced to me as Gina DiBella, Anthony's wife, is looking at me with a lot of interest like she's wondering just how far a man who faced it off with the big boss would feel about testing the old man's nephew, her husband, in some other way . . . like having a go-round with his wife.

I touch the fingertips she holds out to me and do a quick turn away. The young woman of the group is coming our way.

Joseph introduces me to his other nephew, Bruno, his sister's boy and Bruno's fiancée, Angelina Donato.

Neither Bruno or Angelina put out their hands to shake. They just give me this superior going-over with their eyes like a couple of aristocrats inspecting a new horse or dog and Bruno, still looking me over, takes out a hard candy, unwraps it and pops it into his mouth without even offering me one.

"I can't tell you how surprised I was when I found out Vincent passed away," I says.

"It took him sudden," Joseph agreed.

"Heart?" I says.

Anthony makes a rushing sound like he's commenting on what a fool I am. There are people like that who try to make you feel dumb because you don't happen to know something you got no reason to know. You can learn a lot from people like that without even having to ask many questions.

"Vincent was mugged in the park," Joseph said.

Anthony makes the same rushing sound again, softer this time, and Joseph tosses him a look which tells him to watch hisself in front of strangers. I get the feeling that whatever happened to Pastorelli, somebody's going to pay a price.

"Did Vincent have any family?" I asks.

"We was his family," Joseph says.

"Well, I can see he was much loved," I says.

The young woman reaches us and I stand, which courtesy obviously pleases DiBella.

"Mr. Flannery," he says, "I'd like you to meet my wife."

9

I stop over to the Eighteenth District police station on my way home. I know maybe one or two uniforms in the Eighteenth but none of the commanding officers so I ain't sure if it's going to be a waste of time. But I get lucky and bump into one of the cops I know right when I walk through the door.

"Ho, Flannery," Eddie Cascalantti says.

"Ho, Eddie," I says.

"What you doing up in this neck of the woods? I hear you're the new warlord over to the Twenty-seventh. Don't that give you enough to do, or you here to have a look at our toilets?"

"I don't do toilets, Eddie, I only do sewers," I says.

"Big time all the way around, right?" he says.

"You happen to know anything about a bone-breaker by the name of Vincent Pastorelli was found over by Lincoln Park?"

"Chuckie Manoon run that one," he says.

"Chuckie Manoon a cop or a medic?"

"A cop. I don't know what ambulance team run it."

"Chuckie Manoon happen to tell you anything about it?"

"Hit and run. Nothing complicated."

"I wonder could you give me an introduction to Chuckie?"

He turns around and looks at the clock on the wall. "Five minutes," he says. "You hang around five minutes and he should be coming back. I'm going on shift and he's coming off shift. Unless he's otherwise engaged, he'll be walking through that door from the parking bays in five minutes. You could set your watch."

"So, I can afford five minutes."

"You want a cup of coffee and a donut?" Cascalantti asks me as he goes back into the station.

"Weren't you going somewhere when I just bumped into you?" I asks.

"Just going out for a paper. So, we'll have some coffee and chew the fat, then I'll go get the paper."

I have the coffee but do without the donut. Me and Cascalantti sit there chewing the fat. Sure enough this Chuckie Manoon comes through the door from the parking bays right on the button and Cascalantti calls him over and gives me a knockdown to Manoon.

"This is an old friend of mine," Cascalantti tells Manoon. "He wants a little information. Do what you want to do about it but you can take my word for it, Flannery's an ace. You do him a favor and anytime you need it you'll get one back doubled."

"I've got no doubt," Manoon says. "I heard of Flannery."

"Okay, just so you understand he comes with my personal recommendation."

Cascalantti shakes my hand and goes off to start his shift.

"Eddie tells me you was the officer picked up a hit and run by the name of Vincent Pastorelli last week."

Manoon gives me a quirky grin.

"Was there something kinky about it?" I asks.

"I don't know kinky. It was a case of vehicular manslaughter, all right, but I don't know was it an accident."

"How's that?"

"He got hit in the street the first time."

"The first time?"

"The way it looked, whoever hit him chased him up on the grass and hit him again. Knocked him against a tree. That's what killed him."

"So, it was a murder?"

"Hold it. Murder. That's a legal definition carries a lot of weight. Maybe a homicide. Definitely a manslaughter. But I don't know about a murder. The detectives put it down as a hit and run but that could just be they got too many murders on their plate already and didn't want to add to the stats. You know they do that."

"Oh, sure."

"You got a special interest?" he asks.

"The man what was killed was in my night school class."

"That surprises me," Manoon says. "You know what the victim did for a living?"

"Anything illegal. He was a small-time bone-breaker, Carmine DiBella's companion and old goomba."

"That's right."

"Maybe he was retired after Carmine went home to Sicily."

"Well, one way you look at it, he was definitely retired," Manoon says.

"But nobody wants to know for sure."

"Maybe nobody cares."

There's some food for speculation there—like they say—but it ain't enough to keep me thinking about Vincent Pastorelli and his sudden demise or Frank Vollmer and whatever that little toe dance after class was all about, after I get home.

For one thing Kathleen's teething. It was okay with the four little teeth in the front, but now what they call the lateral incisors are coming through and she's in a terrible fret most of the time. After this, Mary tells me, comes the canines and then the first molars, but it's the next several weeks when the pain's going to keep her fussy.

Late at night, when her gums wake her up, I sit in the front room holding her on my lap, listening to some classical music—a little Vivaldi, a little Mozart—and she sucks on my finger which not only soothes her but puts me to sleep. Sometimes I wake up in the morning, stiff as a board, with Kathleen still sleeping in my arms and Mary standing there in her nightdress looking at us both with an expression on her face I can't describe but which makes being a husband and a father—which I don't believe are necessarily the natural state of men—all worthwhile.

Anyways, it's a good thing we can't remember all the pain we went through when we was little.

So, there's that and there's also something that Pothole O'Meara lays on me the other night.

He comes up to me after a class during which we was learning how to parse a sentence, which means breaking it down into its components, and asks me if I got a minute.

"Sure, I always got a minute, Jake," I says.

"I don't live in your ward," he says.

"This a favor you need that I can maybe do for you? Something about a department of the city?"

"I need a little advice, is all," he says.

I give him the nod and says, "That won't cost you nothing."

"Anything," he says, correcting my grammar. He's doing better in class than me.

"Well, how do you know when I say it won't cost you nothing, I don't mean it'll cost you something?"

"Will it cost me something?" he asks.

"No, no," I says. "I was just making a joke. Go ahead. What's the problem?"

"Do you know anything about the arrangement Mrs. Papadopolous set up for her dog?"

"I remember what you said about it the first day of school."

"Well, okay, that was the rough idea. I take care of Billy and we both get to live in the old house in Bridgeport. She left provisions in her will. A trust. The money from the trust pays for the taxes, utilities, food, veterinary, and whatever's left over I split fifty-fifty with her nieces and nephews. I mean the old lady didn't want me to feel like I was on the dole. She wanted me to be able to put a little something away if there was anything left over to put away."

"That was very thoughtful and generous of her," I says.

"That's the way she was. I told her that if she wanted me to take care of Billy when she passed away, I didn't need anything for it. I'd be happy to do it. I used to stop over and see her after she had that run-in with the thief, and Billy and me got to be good friends, so I would've took care—"

"Taken," I says, getting one back.

"—of Billy for nothing. Thanks. You understand what I'm saying?"

"Naturally I understand. I got a dog of my own."

"I had a job. I wasn't just loafing around. I was working security for Acme Guards. Filling in now and then, here and there. I was making enough for what I needed."

I felt like asking just how much that would be since he seemed to have lost all his ambition and given up on life, but that would've been the wrong thing to do. I try not to judge the way people want to run their own lives. Everybody's got their own way to run the race. But it was like he saw the question in my eyes and he goes on.

"All I needed was a little furnished room and a couple of bucks for beans, bread and beer. I didn't have nobody."

"Anybody," I says automatically.

"That's right. Nobody or anybody."

"There's no reason to feel funny about doing what the old lady wanted you to do. I mean it's just as possible that she wanted to make sure old Billy wasn't upset having to move to another house after she died than trying to repay the favor you did for her. So, is there trouble about that?"

"There was plenty of trouble when the will was probated. These nieces and nephews, two of each, raised hell because Mrs. Papadopolous left most of her estate to different charities, churches and hospitals, and there was no way for them to fight big institutions like that in the courts. But they thought they had a shot at getting the house and the trust."

"They working people? I mean could they have used the money?"

"Both nieces is married to very wealthy men. What they would've got from the old lady, even if they got to split up all of it, would be nothing but pin money to them."

"Well, you never know. Some people are putting up a front but there's nothing behind the fancy front door but a pile of bills and no furniture because it's all been sold off."

"Just take my word for it, they're loaded, and their brothers, the old lady's nephews—one's married and one's not—both got more than they know how to spend."

I don't want to go into how much somebody thinks they need or how much they can spend. That's up to the individual, within reason, though I got to admit that I think that these hogs what laugh when you ask them what they want and say, "Everything there is and a little bit more," either have a screw loose or have been raised without much attention to common sense or decency.

"What were they claiming, that you had undue influence on the old woman at the end?" I asks.

"That was the tune they was going to play, but this is four years ago and the house is worth something but not a fortune and the trust is all in very conservative stocks and bonds with the bank as trustee. So they give it up. They figure they'd just wait it out because, except for a stated amount of money which is supposed to come to me as a little cushion for after Billy passes away and I got to leave the house, the house and the rest of the trust goes to them when Billy dies . . . " He turns away and coughs into his hand as though the thought of that moves him. " . . . and I guess they figure they can wait that long to get something they don't really need."

"How come Mrs. Papadopolous didn't leave these nieces and nephews out of her will altogether?"

He shrugs. "She said she wasn't all that fond of her relatives but they was all she had at the end there and what she said to me was, 'Blood's thicker than water,' which I agreed it was."

He coughs again.

"Now we come to the problem. The house all of a sudden triples in value because there's talk of a condo development going into the neighborhood around there. Also one of the stocks in the trust portfolio is this biological engineering stock in this company what develops some new way to make something called Interferon, which they use fighting cancer, and the stock goes through the roof. The pressure's on from these nieces and nephews to get me out of the house so they can sell it before the market collapses and get the trust in their hands so they sell out that stock before somebody else discovers an even better way to make this stuff, in which case the stock could fall."

"I got to tell you, Jake, I'm not the best person in the world in these matters," I says. "It was all I could do to work my way through selling a little piece of property which was left to me and setting up a cooperative purchase of the building me and my wife and kid are presently living in as part owners."

"I ain't asking any financial advice," he says. "The will's been checked and declared legal. There's nothing they can do about that, this late date. What it all turns on now is how long Billy's got to live. He was maybe twelve, thirteen when the old lady died. That's four years ago. So he's maybe sixteen, seventeen now, and any vet'll tell you old Billy ain't long for this world."

"Not a lot you can do about that."

"Nothing I can do about that. But the thing is, they're saying now that Billy could die and I could run out and get another younger dog what looks just like him and stay in the house living high on the hog for another four or five years. I'd just as soon move out and let them have the house. Billy and me could find ourselves a little furnished room somewheres near a park where he could sniff around a little—he don't run much—and I could sit on a bench and get a little sun. Except . . . "

"Except what?" I says when he leaves it dangling there.

"Except it ain't only me and Billy anymore. I been taking stray kids in off the street, giving them a bed, a meal, talking to them about going back home if they're runaways, getting a job if they can't go home. So if Billy goes and I go, they got to go, and I don't know anyplace that's got any room for them. That's why I'm taking this English class. I want to learn how to write better so I can make application for grants and things like that."

"Oh, oh," I says. "You telling me they want to look Billy over? Maybe have their own vet give him a going over, write down everything about him, maybe take a few pictures for purposes of identification?"

"Worse than that. They want to have a number tattooed on Billy's lip so I definitely can't put one over on them."

"Was you . . . were you ready to put one over on them?"

He don't answer me right away.

"Billy's a very old dog," he says as though he's just carefully thought out what he wants to say. "I'm afraid you go sticking a tattoo needle in a dog's mouth that old, the poor animal's going to keel over and die. I take very good care of Billy. That dog could live to be twenty-five."

"So, what you need is a lawyer," I says.

"There's no money I can use for that right at this moment," he says.

"Maybe I can get somebody to do you the favor," I says.

10

The next night I ask Frank Vollmer if I can have a couple of words with him after class.

He says, "Sure. Why don't you tell me what's on your mind while we walk to the parking lot?"

So on the way out there I says, "The reason I wanted to have a couple of words is because an acquaintance of mine is having a little legal difficulty and can't afford a good attorney."

"If he can't afford a good attorney, he certainly can't afford a bad attorney," Vollmer says, making a little lawyer joke there.

"I got to remember that one," I says. "I was wondering if you could . . . "

"My firm does its share of pro bono work," he says. "If you file a brief with the front office secretary—"

"If you'll excuse me," I says, "I'm not asking your firm for the favor. I'm asking you."

He looks at me a little startled and I get it that he's not used to dealing with people one-on-one. He's a corporate lawyer who practically never talks face-to-face with anybody. Not a jury, not a judge and rarely with a client even.

"So, tell me about your acquaintance and the favor you want me to do," Vollmer says as we reach his Jaguar which he's got parked right under a streetlight, a very smart thing to do considering the amount of mugging goes on in dark parking lots.

I give him the rundown of O'Meara and his little problem, Vollmer standing there nodding his head like what I'm telling him is a matter of grave concern.

"Okay. What he needs is a little court injunction. A little cease and desist order. I'll prepare it myself."

"I want to thank you," I says.

Vollmer smiles like he's about to make a joke.

"This favor I'm doing, am I doing it for O'Meara or am I doing it for you?"

"In my situation a favor done for one of my constituents is a favor done for me."

"So he'll owe you and you'll owe me?"

"That's the way it works."

He slaps me alongside the shoulder and says, "I'm only kidding you. No obligation." Then he pauses a second and almost tells me whatever it was he didn't tell me the last time we talked out in the parking lot.

"It's very generous of you to relieve me of any obligation for a quid pro quo," I says, watching his eyebrows shoot up when I give him a little lawyer talk there, "but if ever you need a favor you got a big credit in the book." I tap myself on the forehead, letting him know I got it written down there.

He unlocks the door to his Jaguar and gets in behind the wheel, letting down the electric window to give me a final goodnight. As he drives away it finally hits me that the Jaguar he's driving is the same model I first seen him driving but it ain't the same color. The first time I noticed that it was painted metallic silver-gray and now it's metallic pinkish-white, what they call pearlescent. If you didn't see the paint jobs side by side you could easy think they was the same, especially under the sodium lamps shining down on the parking lot but now that I see the paint jobs are different, I think back and I'd be ready to swear that this wasn't the car he was driving the night he turned the class over to me and was gone for two hours.

When I get home, my father and Mary's mother and Aunt Sada are all sitting around the kitchen table having tea. The three of them hang around a lot together. It looks like when my father married one, he married two.

"We was over to the movie on the avenue and thought we'd stop in and say hello," Mike says.

"We brought a little cake," Aunt Sada says.

"We were waiting for you before we cut it," Charlotte added.

Aunt Sada pops up before Mary and gets the cake out of the fridge.

"A small piece for me, Aunt Sada, and I really mean a small piece," I says.

"Mary still have you on a diet?"

"I haven't got him on anything," Mary protests. "I don't tell James what to do."

Aunt Sada and Charlotte smile at one another like they know better.

"Well, I don't," Mary says, "do I, James?"

"Aaaaah . . ." I says, and everybody has a little laugh. "Anyway, just a little slice. It takes me a lot of work to take a pound off, what with me sitting behind a desk all the time down at work and sitting behind a desk half the time taking care of ward business and sitting in classrooms the rest of the time."

The little speaker in the kitchen—we got one in the living room and our bedroom too—starts peeping like there's a bird in the baby's room, but it's Kathleen waking up and starting to fuss.

"Teething," Mary says, getting up right away to go see.

Aunt Sada follows her, forgetting all about serving the cake, eager for the chance to pick up Kathleen. "You got a little whiskey? A little whiskey on your finger rubbed on her gums'll take away the pain."

"For God's sake, Sada," Charlotte says, following right behind, "what a thing to suggest."

"Mama always used to rub whiskey on our gums when we were teething."

"Who told you that?"

"She did."

"Well, those old-fashioned remedies aren't always very good."

They chatter like that all the way into the baby's

room. We can hear them over the intercom making a quiet fuss over Kathleen.

My father gets up and brings over two slices of cake—a big one for hisself and a small one for me—which Sada has already served out on the plates. I get a couple of forks out of the drawer in the kitchen table.

Mike takes a bite. "Not bad. Not the best, but not bad. Remember the little bakery on the corner when you was a kid where your mother—God rest her soul—would send you over on Saturday mornings to get the baked goods warm from the oven?"

"Streusel cake. Sure I remember."

"That was cake. That bakery's gone now."

"I know. It's been gone for twelve, thirteen years."

"Sure."

He's got a remembering look in his eyes.

"Is it a lot different?" I asks.

"The cake?"

"No. You know. Being married to Charlotte."

"Oh, yes. It's different. It's very quiet."

"Charlotte's very quiet."

"Your mother was quiet. Well, she wasn't always quiet. At least not as quiet as Charlotte. But we was younger and livelier."

I could still hear the ladies in Kathleen's room, but I look over my shoulder and move my chair a little closer anyway before I says, "Before you made the announcement, I sort of had the idea it was Aunt Sada you had an eye for."

"I think maybe I did. She's a lively woman and a lot of fun. I've known a lot of lively women since your mother passed away—may she rest in peace—and I wasn't sure I wanted that twenty-four hours a day. Besides, she's got a lot of opinions and I got a lot of opinions and we would've been arguing all the time. We talked about it, you know."

"Talked about getting married?"

"No, talked about me marrying her sister. I wanted to tell her why I'd picked Charlotte."

"What'd she say?"

"She said she understood and approved. She said Charlotte was a nester and she wasn't, even though she'd been married all those years."

"She didn't get insulted and ask you where you got off thinking you had your pick between them?"

"She's too honest for that, Jimmy. She's a woman what looks a situation over and accepts the possibilities. She said she even gave it some serious thought herself."

"About marrying you?"

"About getting me into bed one night and then making me do the right thing by her."

"Hey, you ain't teenagers. You both been around and these is different times," I says.

"I'm not saying I would've offered but with all of us so close the way we were, I would've done the right thing according to the way I was raised, not according to the way things are nowadays. Running around's no good for anybody, when you get right down to it. There's more hurt than pleasure in it. I mean, look at your friend Vollmer."

"What about my friend Vollmer?"

"There's some words going around that he's a player."

"Couldn't that just be sniping? After all he's an important man and they say he's got political aspirations, so the assassins would be bound to get an early start mixing up some mud pies."

"It could be that, sure. I'm just saying what the word is going around."

11

Somebody says something about an accident, they could mean a thousand things. But, unless they're covering up something else and using one of them euphemisms, when they mention an accident that kills it's either a bad fall or a mechanical wreck like in a plane or car.

Then there's this business of what some people would call coincidence, some people would call the breaks and other people would maybe call intuition. This business about me feeling uneasy over something about Vollmer's Jaguar the night he turned the class over to me and how I notice the color looks different to me the next time I take a good look at it in the school parking lot.

Also, maybe everybody's right when they complain about my curiosity. Maybe I am nosey. Maybe if I'd had the brains for it and a chance for a professional education I could've been a shrink or a psychologist and get paid for poking my nose into other people's business. Of course some people would argue that you invite a shrink or a psychologist to poke around, and I'm always doing it without being asked. I can't deny that.

But what I tell myself I'm doing when I look up the Jaguar dealers in the yellow pages is I'm just checking my memory and my perceptions, a perfectly innocent thing to do.

There's three of them, one in Chicago, one in Elmhurst and one in Palatine.

I call them up one by one and ask them how Mr. Vollmer's car is coming along. The dealer in Chicago and the one in Palatine don't know who I'm talking about. The one in Elmhurst says he's not sure he knows *what* I'm talking about; is Mr. Vollmer not pleased with either of the Jaguars he purchased from the agency at the beginning of the model year?

"Two cars?" I says.

"One for himself and one for Mrs. Vollmer. Who is this, please?" he asks, suddenly getting a little suspicious about somebody asking about a customer who don't seem to know he bought two of them.

"This is Johnny Dark's Detailing Shop," I says, thinking fast. "Mr. Vollmer gave me an order and said I could pick up the car at the dealer's where it was getting some bodywork done."

"Mr. Vollmer told you that?"

"Well, his secretary over to his law office told me that."

"I see what could've happened. She got it wrong. We don't do bodywork here. A customer needs bodywork we either send it over to the service we use if the customer wants us to pick up the vehicle, or we give the customer the recommendation if he wants to handle it himself."

"Well, that's it then. You mind giving me the name of the body shop?"

"Why not? It's Devon Downs Restorations."

"You happen to have the address handy?"

He rattles off an address on North Elston over by the John Kennedy Expressway.

It's got a fancy name and works on fancy cars, but a body shop's a body shop, always noisy and everybody in it greasy and short-tempered.

When it's plain to the guy with MAC embroidered on the pocket of his coverall, that I'm not a new customer but maybe somebody come to complain about not getting a car when promised or at the very least somebody who's going to waste his time asking questions, he stands there wiping his hands on a greasy rag ready to be unpleasant.

"What do you know," I says. "Anybody ever tell you how much you look like Burt Reynolds?"

He looks about as much like Burt Reynolds as my left foot, but the flattery's enough to thaw him out in a second. It ain't only women what like to be told they look good.

"Well not lately," he says, touching his hair. "It's getting a little thin on top."

I pat my stomach, "Well if it ain't one thing, it's another. That's a good-looking Jaguar you got over there. I like the color."

He looks at the metallic silver-gray XKJ Jag, which is being hand buffed after coming out of the infrared oven that takes up the whole back of the shop, and says, "That metallic's hard to get just right. A whole fender or a side panel's not so bad but you got rear end or front end damage that makes it so you got to match it up, it's hard getting it to match up without you can see the ghost of an overlap. You know what I mean?"

"How about you paint the whole car?"

"That costs like hell. Most customers won't pay for perfect."

"That one looks perfect. Did that customer pay for perfect?"

"That customer always pays for perfect. He's a lawyer. You know what I'm saying?"

"He can afford it."

"He'll get it out of the next poor sucker what walks into his office looking for some advice."

"So, was that a rear end or a front end?" I asks.

"Wiped out the hood and windshield. Said he hit a deer over to the Forest Preserve."

"I didn't know there was that many deer over to the Forest Preserve."

"Well, there was one," he says. "Blood smeared all over the front."

He's smiling, he's being chatty, but he's also looking me over a little close.

"You didn't say what I can do for you," he says.

"I'm afraid to ask," I says.

"So, ask."

I walk outside where I got my Chevy parked and he walks out with me.

"I was driving by and saw your shop and all of a sudden I wondered just how much it'd cost to give the old heap a paint job."

"You said it," he says.

"Said what?"

"You called it a heap. I don't want to hurt your feelings—"

"Don't worry, I know it ain't a beauty."

"—but it ain't worth a paint job. If you got to have one, try any of the Earl Scheibs, a hundred and forty-nine bucks for a quick enamel."

"Well, it was just a thought," I says. "Thanks for the chat."

I get in my car and drive off as he stands there watching me, wondering if all I wanted was to find out what a paint job for an old car would cost. Then he shrugs and tucks the rag into his back pocket and I know he's not going to call Vollmer about somebody coming around asking idle questions. He's just going to forget all about it.

12

Janet Canarias stops in to see me Monday night while I'm listening to all the precinct captains bringing me the troubles and sorrows of their neighbors. It feels all right because I'm helping people what need help and I guess I'm one of those do-gooders and busybodies that arrogant people like to sneer at and make jokes about, but it ain't really the same as when I used to walk around my precinct, put my foot up on the steps to the porch or sit on the stoop and chew the fat. Except people sit out on the porches and stoops less and less nowadays. I keep forgetting that.

She gives me a kiss on the cheek and I ask her how come she ain't been stopping by the last week, ten days.

She makes a motion like she's cutting her pretty throat and says, "Because I've been up to here, Jimmy."

"Anything special?"

"Everything's special, isn't it, Jimmy? I mean every

person that comes to us with a problem thinks it's something special. And little things that pop that don't seem important at first glance turn out to be very, very important. I'm reminded . . . "

I wait for her to tell me what she's reminded about. The nice thing with certain old friends is that the conversation don't go in a straight line. One thought don't have to be finished before you're off on another, bouncing around from one thing to another, because you know each other so well that you can fill in the blanks and see every wild connection.

"You remember years ago there was a boss back in Jersey City, New Jersey?" she asks.

"Sure. Frank Hague."

"I was reading a book about big city bosses the other day and a quote attributed to him stuck in my mind," she says. "I probably won't get it exactly right but apparently when somebody accused him of being a crook he replied, 'I ain't going to argue that with you, because I can see your mind's already made up. But if you're right and I am a crook, then all I got to say is there's only one crook in Jersey City.'"

"I see his point," I says.

"So do I. That's why the quotation stuck. He was asking this critic which he'd rather have and what was better for the people, a bunch of crooks out there fighting over the graft or one powerful boss, who would probably steal a lot less than a hundred wanting to be just like him."

"You want a cup of coffee?" I asks.

"Tea would be nicer," she says.

"I can do that."

"Can you do herb tea?"

I go over to the sideboard where I got a pot of coffee and a pot of hot water always going on the double hot plate. I look through a box of mixed tea packets.

"I got orange spice. I got camomile. I got lemon mint. I got—"

"You're a regular health food bar."

"—vanilla cinnamon."

"Orange spice."

I turn the heat up under the water and says, "Only take a second. Got to get the water rolling. My mother—God rest her soul—always used to say that was the big mistake people what wasn't Irish made when they was making tea, they never got the water up to a rolling boil. So . . . ?"

"I just got word from an inside source that Wally Dunleavy's right-hand man, Lou Kibby's, going to leak a little story about some old-fashioned patronage and municipal sinecures."

"People getting paid without doing any work?"

"That's right."

"In Streets and Sanitation?"

"That's right."

"Who?"

"Don't ask me who," she says. "Ask me how many."

"How many," I says.

"Forty-eight. That's the number of those investigated and uncovered."

"I don't think I want to ask the next question," I says.

"I know what you're thinking. These freeloaders aren't in the Twenty-seventh, they're in the First."

"So, they're not after . . . ?"

"After you or anybody you know?"

"I was going to say you."

"No, they're not after me. I don't think they're really after anybody in particular."

"So, what are they after?"

"The problem of unemployment. Look," she says, "these are very hard times. The federal government cuts funding to the states at the same time they go mandating new and more inclusive social programs."

"Laying off the burden on the nearest donkey," I says.

"But the states aren't the last donkeys."

"That would be the counties and cities."

"So the mayors have the final burden of funding and staffing these programs with, nowadays, increasing unemployment in the private sector and decreasing tax revenues in spite of tax increases, which sends businesses and the middle classes running elsewhere."

"And there's a lot of pressure from people to who—whom?—favors are owed what got friends and relatives without jobs. But hiding forty-eight freeloaders ain't easy."

"Practically all of them are in the Parking Bureau. You could hide a hundred and forty-eight sleeping bodies in the public garages if you wanted to."

"So, if they could hide these people without much chance of getting caught, why's the leak coming out of Dunleavy's office, right from the top? They ain't—"

"Trying to force the old man to finally take retirement? Force him out with a little scandal?"

"He'd never allow it. Anybody ever dared to pull a

stunt like that on Dunleavy, heads would roll and buildings would burn."

"Don't you get it?" Janet asks.

The water's boiling, so I pour some over a teabag in a mug, bring it back to the desk and put it in front of Janet, which gives me time to work it through in my head.

"It come down from the fifth floor?" I asks.

"That's right. The order to leak the story of this flagrant example of nepotism, this outrageous abuse of office, this taint of civic corruption came from the mayor's office or someplace very nearby."

"Why else would Lou Kibby betray the old man for whom—who?—he'd cut off his left arm?"

"And who else would volunteer to be the sacrificial lamb for the sake of the administration and the party but an old man who'll retire or die within the year, whichever comes first."

"But I still don't see the keeno."

Janet taps the side of her nose. "Neither do I. Not yet. But something's getting ripe."

"Well," I says, smiling at her like one partner to the other, "you and I—me—'ll have to keep our eyes peeled."

"You're going to have to stop doing that, Jimmy," she says.

"Doing what?"

"Correcting yourself all the time."

"Well, that's why I'm taking the class in grammar, ain't it—isn't it?"

"I liked it better when Mary and me—I—did it for you," she says, and we both have a laugh.

13

On Saturday afternoon I'm over to Brennan's Tavern as usual, ready to lend a helping hand or at least a sympathetic ear to any of my precinct captains what—which? that?—got a problem.

I got Alfie with me. He likes his little outing now and then and we ride along sometimes making believe we're a couple of fellas on their own without a worry in the world. Men and dogs got to make believe like that every once in a while if they want to stay sane. Women, too.

I tell Brennan to lay out a selection of sandwiches, corned beef on rye, ham and cheese on whole wheat, like that.

"How about some tuna salad?" Brennan asks. "I made a nice tuna salad this morning. You could have it on sourdough."

"What's with the sourdough? What is this, San Francisco?" I asks. "Never mind the tuna anyway. If they don't get et—"

"Eaten," Brennan says.

"—the bread gets soggy and they won't keep when I got to take the leftovers home." I don't say anything about the fact that he just corrected my grammar.

What we got here is a conspiracy to drive me nuts. Ever since friends, neighbors, colleagues and constituents got wind of the fact that I'm taking an English class, everybody gets the idea that they got the right to correct every little thing I say.

Just the other day Packy Cooley and me have a discussion what lasts twenty, thirty minutes about the use of was and were like if you said, "It was as though" or "It were as though" and another half hour about when it's supposed to be "I" and when it's supposed to be "me."

This Saturday nobody arrives to consult with me except Packy Cooley. Maybe that's because the Cubs are playing a very important game, maybe it's because nobody's got any big problems, the weather being fine and the streets in reasonably good repair. Most of the requests a precinct captain gets—except for hardship cases—is about cutting the limbs off shade trees what are blocking the sun into somebody's apartment and fixing the potholes in the street.

At first I'm afraid that Cooley wants to have another discussion about the English language but instead he tells me about one of the people in his precinct, a woman by the name of Donna Mendoza, a hardworking woman who's afraid she's going to lose her job working as an attendant in one of the municipal parking lots because word's out that there could be an investigation into certain abuses whereby employees punch in, then go to another job elsewhere before coming back after five to punch out.

"Has she been accused of this?" I asks.

"Not yet, but she says she knows it's going to happen because her supervisor's got it in for her because she objects when he tries to pat her on the ass—"

"She's got a case of sexual harassment there," I says.

"—and he'd like to do her an injury. What are you talking about? How's she going to prove something like that? Even if she could how can she afford to have it on her sheet that she's a troublemaker? How can she afford to be without a salary while they screw around looking into the situation, which could take three or four months?"

"All right. I understand what you're saying. I'll go have a talk. You say she works at the Parking Bureau?"

"Facilities."

"Who's the boss? Not her boss, the top boss."

"His name is Hruska. He's a Slovak. If I was you I'd go over his head to the top. I'd go right to Dunleavy."

Which is my intention.

"Were," I says.

"What were?" he says.

"If I were you I'd go and so forth," I says.

"If I *was* you," he says. "Singular."

"If I were you. Future probable," I says, making up a little razzle-dazzle there.

"If I was you," Cooley says.

So I say, "Okay, if it makes you feel better. Go have a sandwich and a beer and see who else wants to see me."

"You see anybody else wants to see you?"

He goes over to the bar and has his beer and sandwich and then he leaves.

So I—me—I and Alfie sit around for an hour more
and when nobody else shows up I ask Brennan how
many sandwiches he made and he tells me twenty-five.

"You think you could sell them to your lunch
trade?" I ask him.

"Hey, I got a reputation. I can't go selling sandwiches I already got made to my customers who are
expecting me to build them to order."

"Who'd know the difference?"

"I'd know the difference. I made them for your
bunch, Flannery, and I'm afraid you got to pay for
them and eat them here or take them home with you."

"I'm glad I didn't let you make the tunas," I says.

I'm not about to take home twenty-five sandwiches
with meat in them, especially since Mary decides we
should eat more vegetarian and it's all I can do to get a
piece of meat on the table. So I eat three of the corned
beef on rye right there in Brennan's, washed down
with a glass of root beer from the keg. Brennan's is the
only place in town that still serves root beer from the
wood. Where he gets it I don't know and he won't tell.
And I give Alfie the meat from another one even
though Mary would have something to say about that,
too.

Anyway, I take the twenty-one sandwiches left over
with me and decide they'd make a nice treat for the
kids in O'Meara's halfway house.

I got the address over in Bridgeport in my address
book and it don't take me more than fifteen minutes
to drive over there.

It's the biggest house on the block and it looks to me like somebody's painted it lately, so old Mrs. Papadopolous's nieces and nephews can't claim that O'Meara ain't took—taken—good care of their property which ain't going to be their property until the old dog, Billy, dies.

I park in front of the house and Alfie gives me the old eye, trying to figure am I going to leave him waiting in the car the way I do sometimes.

I go around and open the door on the passenger side and he jumps out, glad of the opportunity to do a little socializing. I mean, dogs are like men that way, too.

"There's somebody I'd like you to meet," I says.

Alfie wags his tail and we go trotting up the path to the porch steps, me with the sack of Brennan's sandwiches under my arm.

The front door to the vestibule's open. The door to the foyer's got a big oval piece of glass in it and I can see somebody at a desk under the staircase leading upstairs. I just walk in without even knocking because there's something about the house that has the personality of a public place.

The person at the desk looks up and I can see it's Miss Esper, my English teacher.

"Well, hello, Jimmy, what brings you here?"

"About twenty sandwiches came my way and I thought maybe Mr. O'Meara and his youngsters would appreciate them. Also I'd like to have a talk with him about something he asked me to do."

"Billy," she says, looking down at Alfie, "go see if you can find Jake."

Alfie goes over to her wagging his tail, ready to get a pet, him always being one who likes the attentions of a pretty woman.

"You're not Billy," she says when Alfie gets closer.

"That's my dog, Alfie," I says. "Does Jake's dog look like Alfie?"

"Well, it would be easy to make the mistake, just as I did," she says, "but now that Alfie's come closer I can see that Alfie's a much younger dog."

She stops petting Alfie and stands up, looking very attractive in a man's shirt tied off over a bare midriff, a pair of faded jeans and Indian moccasins on her feet.

I don't know if she reads my mind but she holds out her arms a little bit, like she's displaying her clothes, and says, "I help Mr. O'Meara out when I can, and you've got to be dressed, ready to do anything, around here."

"I saw the paint job," I says.

"Jake thought it would be a good idea to spruce the place up a little. We're supposed to be having visitors from the court."

"Does Jake have a budget to maintain the house?"

"Oh, yes, but he wouldn't spend it on something like painting and repairs when we can do it ourselves. I was slinging a brush," she says with some pride, "but I didn't go up on the ladders. Jake and the boys and girls did that."

"You got both living here?"

"Both what?"

"Boys and girls."

"Why not?"

"I don't know, I just thought you got boys and girls

with problems living in the same house they're maybe going to form relationships."

"That would be a very good thing, don't you think? Most of the time the reason why these kids end up out on the streets is because they couldn't handle relationships. You want me to take that paper sack off your hands?"

I hand over the bag of sandwiches.

"There's corned beef and ham and cheese," I says. "I hope this house ain't vegetarian?"

She laughs. "Everybody around here is an omnivore as far as I can tell. You want a tour?"

"Sure, why not?" I says.

"I'll show you around. We'll bump into Jake somewhere."

We drop the food off in the kitchen where there's a couple of nice-looking kids, a boy and a girl about fifteen, sixteen, chopping up some vegetables.

"Donations," Cora says, holding up the paper sack. Then she introduces everybody all around, using just first names. "You can serve them for lunch and save the stew for supper," she says and we go upstairs by way of a staircase that leads off a laundry room next to the kitchen where two more kids are sorting through some clothes.

Alfie gives the food on the table a sniff—the sandwiches, not the vegetables—but decides it's beneath his dignity to hang around strangers looking for a handout, so he trots upstairs at our heels.

O'Meara's up in the attic with a couple of lanky kids, painting the new walls he's just put up. It looks like he intends to expand operations, turning the attic into a dormitory which'll be able to sleep maybe eight or nine more runaways and strays.

There's a dog laying on the scrubbed pine floors in a patch of sunshine coming in through the window. If I didn't know better, and if Alfie didn't go trotting over to exchange calling cards, I would've believed it was Alfie hisself.

"Look at that, will you," O'Meara says coming over to touch my elbow with his elbow because his hands are covered in paint.

"They could be brothers," I says.

"More like father and son. Billy's a lot older."

"Anyway they belong to the same clan," I says.

Which is pretty obvious. There's a breed of mutt— what some people would call a lovely mixed breed— which seems to occupy a niche in the ecology of every city I've ever been in. They're usually a patchy black and white, about twenty pounds, with a long shaggy tail and blue eyes what look almost human, very intelligent and easygoing but able to take care of themselves if they got to. We've all seen a thousand of them and here's two more.

"Did a lawyer by the name of Frank Vollmer get in touch with you?" I says.

"Yes, thank you very much, Jimmy," O'Meara says. "He called to say you'd asked him to look into the business of Billy getting tattooed and told us not to worry, he'd take care of it the first chance he got."

"So he took care of it?"

"Sent the necessary constraint order by messenger yesterday afternoon," Cora says.

"Oh?" I says. "You don't happen to have it handy, do you?"

"It's in my desk," she says. "I can go downstairs and get it."

"I'll go down with you. I just stopped by to say hello and see if everything was all right."

"It's as right as it'll ever be as long as those relatives of Mrs. Papadopolous are on my back," O'Meara says. "Besides trying to tattoo Billy, they're trying to stir up the neighbors about me running a boarding house without a permit."

"Well, I'll look up the regulations on that, too, if you want me to," I says.

"That would be much appreciated," O'Meara says.

"Okay, then," I says, "say good-bye, Alfie. We're going."

We go downstairs and Cora gets the constraint order from the desk drawer.

"You wouldn't happen to have the envelope it come in, would you?" I asks.

"We save everything around here," she says. She goes into another drawer and comes out with one of them envelopes with the string tie and the holes punched in it. "There's the record of the time the envelope was picked up on the ripoff receipt. Three twenty on Friday afternoon."

"I wonder could I use the phone?" I says. "It's a local call."

"Help yourself. I'll go into the kitchen and make some iced tea. You want to stay and have one of those sandwiches you brought?"

"I already had three."

"A glass of iced tea, then?"

"I don't think so, thanks. I'll just make this call and then Alfie and me—I'll—be on our way."

She walks away smiling because I corrected myself and she knows her teaching ain't going entirely to waste.

I call up a friend of mine at City Hall and get the address of Frank Vollmer over in Roger's Park—in the Twenty-fourth Ward—since I already looked him up in the phone book and find out he ain't listed.

I thank him and tell him that I owe him one—which he says, "Don't worry, I just wrote it down in the book."

"I hope you wrote it in small numbers," I says, and we have a laugh.

14

Sure enough, just like Janet Canarias predicted, Lou Kibby leaks the story about city workers what ain't working.

I'm sitting in the outer office waiting to see Wally Dunleavy when the media comes swarming in asking for—no, demanding—an interview, a defense and an explanation.

Dunleavy hisself comes toddling out, all smiles, to meet the members of the press, radio and television, the "all-smelling nose, all-hearing ear and all-seeing eye" as Dunleavy calls them in greeting just to put everybody into a jolly mood. He spots me and sings out, "Jimmy Flannery. James, my boy, is it me you're waiting to see?" as though he's a humble man, about to be cast aside, past usefulness and pitifully grateful that he still has somebody in his outer office waiting to see him. "Come with me," he says, throwing an arm around my shoulder as I stand up to shake his hand. "There's not a reason in the world why one of my oldest and dearest friends shouldn't sit in on this public statement I've been asked to make. Maybe you can even protect me from these sweet people who'd have my liver."

Dunleavy, as you can see, is a master at sticking in the knife, insulting people to their faces, and making them like it. He's using the principle that insulting your friends is a sign of affection and if anybody present takes exception to his remarks it automatically signifies that they don't consider themselves friends of his and then they better watch out.

On the way through the maze of corridors, created over the years out of these portable office panels that're supposed to make temporary cubicles for office workers, he's kissing this lady on the cheek and slapping this guy on the back, calling them by name and asking about the wives, husbands and kiddies.

By the time we reach his office, even though it's a long way to lunchtime, his staff has set out a couple of trays of sandwiches, one of them forty-cup coffeemakers and several bottles of wine.

I can hardly believe my eyes. His desk and every other table in the room, which are usually ten inches deep in plans and maps, ashtrays full of cigar butts and empty cans of iced tea, are as clean as a whistle except for the refreshments.

He steps over behind his desk, splays out his fingers on the desk top, leans forward a couple of inches, smiles sweetly and says, "Would you like me to be sitting or standing?"

"Make yourself comfortable, Commissioner," Donny Mulholland from the *Chicago Trib* says. Being the senior newsperson on the story he just sort of takes over at being the one who'll do the courtesy bits with Dunleavy.

Dunleavy sweeps one arm out, indicating the food and drink. "Help yourself," he says, which they are already doing. He tosses out the other arm and says, "Pick a pew."

I don't sit down. I go stand in the back of the room where I can lean against the doorjamb if the performance goes on too long.

"Would it be okay," he says, "if I make a statement before you start asking me your questions?"

"Go right ahead, Your Honor," Mulholland says, sitting right down front with two sandwiches in one hand and a plastic cup of wine in the other.

"Well, thank you, Donny," Dunleavy says, "for making me a judge. I ain't your honor, all I am is an old engineer doing the best he can to keep the bowl of spaghetti which is the streets and parks and this and that of this great city straightened out the best way I know how.

"In order to accomplish this great task we got departments. We got departments of Central Complaint and Inquiry, the Electricity Bureau, the Bureau of Equipment Services, Electrical Wire and Communications, the Rodent Control Bureau, the Street Operations Bureau and we got the Bureau of Parking and Parking Facilities.

"Under the last we got the Office of Traffic Rules and Regs, Parking Facilities, Lots and Curbs, Meters and Fees . . ."

He names every division, department, bureau, office

and closet in his domain. By this time a couple of the ladies are getting giddy and Jock Harrigan from the *Sun-Times*, well known for his early start on the day's drinking, is ready to fall asleep.

Finally, having never mentioned a word about what brings all these news types to his office, he launches into a history of parking meters.

"I was never a great believer in parking meters," he says. "There's something undignified about grown men and women running down the street to feed quarters into a metal box so the meter police don't give them a ticket for overtime. They're an offense to the principle of the commons by which the public squares, parks, streets, avenues, alleys and byways are there for the use of all."

Everybody's giving each other the eye, wondering what the hell the old man's dithering on about. You can see they're wondering if he's finally tipped over the edge into senility, having hung on to his appointment longer than anybody in modern history.

"It starts out that meters are justified for the control of parking in business districts for the benefit of the merchants, who desire a steady flow of customers, and for the public, too, who want at least a fighting chance to find a parking space on the street if they got to run into a shop for a tube of toothpaste or a new set of underwear . . . "

Whaaaaat, you could practically hear everybody saying.

"In the beginning the excuse is traffic flow and the continuous availability of parking spaces but before you know it the city starts depending on the revenue.

So the reason for parking meters ain't the same anymore. The whole scheme becomes a cash cow.

"Now where you got a cash cow you got a lot of cats coming around for a taste—"

"Which brings us to the forty-eight city employees in question?" Mulholland says.

"Which brings us there," Dunleavy says, smiling benignly on one and all. He leans forward. "Now, how the hell am I supposed to keep track of a handful of meter readers out of maybe six thousand employees in my organization? That's not an excuse, it's an observation."

"What's being done about it?" Shirley Ostrowski from the ABC television station asks.

"I've already launched a full-scale investigation, Shirley. I've already suspended the forty-eight persons accused and their supervisor."

"Who is?"

"Who will remain nameless. None of us wants to try and condemn a servant of the people in the press, do we?"

"How about your deputy in charge of Parking Facilities?" somebody else asks.

"On notice."

"Is he running the investigation?"

"He is cooperating with an independent referee already assigned by the mayor's office."

"Even if this present situation is cleared up to the public satisfaction," Mulholland says, "what guarantees does the public have that such abuses won't occur again?"

Dunleavy smiles like he's overjoyed somebody

should have asked that question. You could practically see him tip old Donny Mulholland the wink, thanking him for doing what they'd clearly agreed he would do.

"I'm making a recommendation that metering, lot attendance and other services related to traffic, parking and other public concerns be taken out of civil service and placed into the hands of private operators where the job can be done more efficiently and to the greater profit of all."

So there it was. The fuse that Janet Canarias suspected had been lit when she mentioned the leak about a patronage scandal coming out of the mayor's office by way of Lou Kibby just set off the firecracker.

There's some more questions and then we're alone, Dunleavy and me.

We're looking at what they left behind. The trays of sandwiches have been picked clean; they ain't left a crumb. The wine bottles have disappeared. The forty-cup stainless steel coffeemaker's still there.

"I guess the coffeemaker was too hot to stick under their coat," Dunleavy says. "So what did you come to see me about, Flannery?"

"I guess I already heard the answer to my question."

"What's your interest?"

"One of the people under the gun is from my ward. She's not the type to sign in and then leave the job."

"She got a name?"

"Donna Mendoza."

He writes down the name.

"You tell her to report to this office tomorrow morning and we'll find something for her to do."

He looks very old and very tired.

"Why'd they ask you to let them use your domain to run their keeno?" I asks.

"Can I tell you something in confidence, Flannery?"

"Nobody ever has to ask can I keep a confidence."

"That's what I been told. The end of this month, right after this minor drama is over, I'm finally going to do what a hundred friends have advised me to do and ten thousand enemies have wanted me to do for more than a decade. I'm hanging up my guns, Jimmy."

"You and Delvin can sit around in the parks, maybe over to the zoo, watching the skirts of the young women blowing around their legs, telling each other war stories."

"You couldn't get old Delvin out of his parlor with a stick of dynamite," Dunleavy says. "Anything else, Jimmy?"

"I'm glad I stopped by to say hello, Mr. Dunleavy. It's been a pleasure knowing you." I go over and shake his hand, thinking there are a couple of things I'd like to know. For one thing, I'd like to know how far this privatization movement is going to spread after this trial balloon. For another, I'd like to know who's going to be in charge of letting out the contracts.

But I don't ask. I just shake Dunleavy's old hand and wonder how long it's going to be before some young guy is shaking mine.

I drive away thinking about what I know or think I know.

Frank Vollmer bought two Jaguars, one for hisself and one for somebody other than his wife.

Frank Vollmer wrecked the front end of his Jaguar the night he left the class and Pastorelli followed him.

Pastorelli was killed in an accident.

Frank Vollmer was driving a different Jaguar the last time I see him because his Jaguar's in the shop getting some bodywork and a new paint job.

What I don't know is what the hell I can do with the information.

It's while I'm on the way home that the news comes over the radio that Joan Vollmer, Frank Vollmer's wife's, condition ain't improved; she's still in a coma.

Sometimes you get so busy that you can't keep up with what's going on in the world, even in your own hometown, even with people you know. I didn't even know about Mrs. Vollmer being in any coma. I don't know how long she's been there. I don't know what caused it.

15

Frank Vollmer naturally ain't at school Thursday, which is the next night. A substitute comes in to take over and says something vague about the "other instructor," meaning Vollmer, having an emergency or a tragedy or something in the family. This man's name is Horace Pendergast and I got the feeling he stopped paying attention to world affairs about the time of the Spanish-American War. We hear a lot about Teddy Roosevelt and William Randolph Hearst.

When I get home, Mary tells me that Jake O'Meara called and asked me to call him back.

Which I do. One of the kids gets on the phone, grunts at me when I ask him to go get O'Meara. I'm standing there waiting so long that I'm starting to wonder if the kid actually went to tell O'Meara he's wanted on the phone. Kids that age forget what they're doing walking from here to there.

Finally O'Meara's on the phone.

"What can I do for you, Jake?" I asks.

"Well, I ain't really sure."

"So, tell me the problem and we'll go from there."

"The nieces and nephews are coming over with their lawyer to look Billy over."

"You told them about the order to cease and desist?"

"They said they ain't got any intention of laying a finger on Billy."

"They ain't bringing a vet?"

"They said they just wanted their attorney to assess the situation. I think what they want is to have him try and talk me into a settlement and take a walk. Leave the house and trust to them and get it over with."

"So, you tell them no if you want to tell them no."

"I'm going to do that, but what I'm worried about is Billy ain't feeling so good and they'll see that. They'll be around all the time if they think Billy's about ready to die and that's not going to do me or the kids any good. I mean these kids get the idea what they got here is ready to bust apart, and they'll just scatter."

"That's going to happen sooner or later, ain't it?" I says.

"I'm working on a couple of whatayacallits."

"What's that?"

"You know. Standbys. As, Bs and Cs."

"Contingency plans?"

"That's right."

"When are they due to arrive?"

"Saturday noon."

"Well, I got to tell you the truth, Jake, I don't know what we can cook up on such short notice."

"I had sort of an idea."

"What's that?" I asks.

"I thought maybe we could switch dogs."

"Switch dogs?"

"You know. I could take Alfie and you could take Billy. Just until they got a gander at Alfie and saw what good shape he's in."

"Thinking it's Billy?"

"That's right."

"You think it'll fool them? Alfie and Billy look a lot alike, but up close—"

"Billy never lets any of them get near him. He knows what's what and shows them his teeth. It'll work."

I'm trying to figure out how deceitful, even unethical, this thing he's asking me to do would measure on a scale of one to ten compared to the damage that these nieces and nephews are trying to do to O'Meara.

"It ain't exactly dishonest," O'Meara says, like he could read my mind.

"It's something to think about, though."

"Well, I can understand that," he says, sounding disappointed, sounding like he thinks I'm letting him down.

"Let me get back to you," I says. "I got to have a consultation with somebody. Give me fifteen minutes."

I hang up and see that Mary's looking at me from where she's sitting at the kitchen table like she's ready to advise and consent.

"You'll excuse me if I don't ask your opinion on this one," I says.

"You going to call your father?"

"I don't think so."

"It's a little late to be calling an old man like Mr. Delvin."

"Well, I wasn't thinking about calling him either," I says. "I figure you need an expert in a situation like this." I start dialing a number. "I'm going to see if Willy Dink's at the all-night diner where he gets his messages."

Willy Dink is an old friend of mine who lives in a trailer he built hisself on the back of an old pickup truck with a chicken, a ferret, a king snake, a rat terrier by the name of Timmy, an armadillo and a couple of other creatures which are partners in his business. He advertises hisself as the only Natural and Organic Vermin and Rodent Exterminator in Chicago.

A couple of years ago he helped me out and I repaid the favor by getting him a job with the city as a consultant but that didn't last too long since Willy Dink's a very independent person who finds it impossible to work inside any set of rules and regulations.

He is also somebody whose word is truly, actually and legitimately his bond, which is something you don't get a lot of nowadays.

He comes to the phone and gives me his spiel about his nonpolluting, nonpoisonous, guaranteed biodegradable extermination service before I can interrupt him long enough to tell him it's me, Jimmy Flannery, on the phone and I know his pitch as good as he knows it.

"Long time no see," he says.

"Well, it's been a lot of this and that," I says.

"Ups and downs?"

"Ins and outs."

"I get a lot of that in my business," he says. "What can I do you for?"

"I'm faced with an ethical problem," I says.

"Give me the facts," he says.

I lay out O'Meara's dilemma for him. How he's trying to protect the welfare of this old dog. How these greedy relatives are trying to move in and maybe do the dog an injury or at the very least put the old mutt through considerable distress. How the dog, Billy, is feeling poorly and the relatives are coming over with a lawyer to inspect the premises and the dog. How O'Meara figures they'll be haunting the house if they see that Billy's maybe on his last leg, so he's asking me to put Alfie in as a stand-in for Billy just until the inspection tour is over.

"So, what's the problem?" Willy Dink says. "You got an animal threatened here. It's one of them situations where you got to look at the greater good."

"You mean I got to ask myself is it in the greater good not to throw in a ringer with the intent to deceive and defraud or is it for the greater good to do what has to be done to save Billy from this distress?"

I'm looking at Mary out of the corner of my eye. She's got this little smile on her face.

"You just summed it up exactly," Willy Dink says, "so you got your answer."

"Protect Billy."

"No question."

"Only there's one problem."

"What's that?"

"Billy don't like these relatives, won't go near them

and won't let them get near him. Shows his teeth when and if they try."

"That dog's no fool."

"Well, Alfie's got no reason to growl at these people and, smart as he is, I don't think I can say to him, 'Alfie, there's going to be these four or five people coming into O'Meara's house and I want you to growl at them so they can't get close enough to see that you ain't Billy.'"

"I see the problem," Willy Dink says and then he's quiet for a minute. "When does this performance take place?" he finally asks.

"Saturday noon."

"That should give us plenty of time."

"Time for what?"

"I got to make a call to a friend of mine over to the zoo."

"The zoo?"

"I'm going to get you a little something. You spread a little bit on a glove and when these people come to see the dog you shake everybody's hand. They won't be able to get within five feet of Alfie or any other dog."

"What's this stuff I'm going to be putting on a glove?"

"Lion shit," Willy Dink says.

16

Janet Canarias calls me at work on Friday morning and asks me what I think of the mayor's announcement.

"What announcement?" I says.

"It was on the seven o'clock local news," she says.

"I was down in manhole number thirty-three checking some valves at seven o'clock this morning," I says, "so I was out of touch."

"You want to have lunch?" she asks me.

"Say where and when."

"One o'clock at the hot dog by the Red Dog."

I know she means the outdoor sausage vendor in the Richard J. Daley Plaza where Picasso's big hunk of sculpture some people call the Red Dog and which is supposed to look like Picasso's wife and also his Russian wolfhound sits.

I'm there ten minutes early because I know she's always on the minute and I want to have our lunch ready so she don't have to wait in line.

I get her a Polish sausage and a Milwaukee beer. I get myself a Polish and a root beer.

"Well, the mayor pulled it off."

"Pulled what off?"

"Some sleight of hand. You remember how we talked about the federal government cutting funding on the one hand and mandating more social programs and services to the states with the other?"

I tell her I remember very well, though I got to admit politics on the national level don't interest me all that much except when it starts making the city's shoes pinch. Which apparently it's doing.

"You remember how we talked about how the states had to look to the cities and counties to take on more and more of the burden?"

I say I do.

"Which leaves a lot of towns, including Chicago, with swollen bureaucracies, too many civil servants, overloaded payrolls. Well, the mayor just announced that the parking lots, garages and curbside metering of the city is being privatized. First of all he cuts the scandal about payroll padding and double-dipping workers in the bud. Secondly, he takes the burden of a huge bureaucracy off his shoulders. Thirdly, he has some very important contracts to give out. And lastly, he'll be able to go to the people and say that he's reduced the cost of government."

"By firing five, six thousand city workers."

"He won't take the hit for that. The private contractor who takes over the running of the facilities will have to weather that storm. The mayor can simply look on with sadness, regret and dismay."

"Who'll get the job of handing out the contracts?" I asks.

"The Municipal Pier, Canal, Garages, Public Curbs and Expansion Agency."

"Frank Vollmer," I says.

"Well, that part of it," she says. "I suppose it doesn't really matter who hands out the pork."

"I don't know about that," I says, thinking about the fact that it probably means a lot to Frank Vollmer.

We sit there chewing on our sausages and eyeing the big red chunk of steel.

"What do you think it looks like?" I asks.

"What looks like?"

"Picasso's statue. You think it looks more like his wife or his dog?"

"I'd put my money on the dog," she says.

17

It takes me until Friday night to find out that nobody else knows what caused Mrs. Vollmer's illness either. Not yet. At least nobody's saying. When I ask Mary to bend the rules a little and see what she can find out about Mrs. Vollmer's condition from her friend Sylvia Klein, the supervising nurse over to Illinois Masonic, all she can get is that Joan Vollmer was found unconscious sometime Thursday night when her husband came home from a business dinner, she was admitted on Friday afternoon under a blanket of secrecy and her condition is stable though she's still unresponsive.

"Did your friend say what put her into the coma?" I asks.

"She didn't know. Mrs. Vollmer's physician is keeping the chart and just giving out separate instructions four times a day," Mary says, "but my friend has suspicions—more than suspicions—that the coma was induced by an overdose of barbiturates in combination with some other drug or drugs."

"A suicide attempt?"

"Well, she didn't go so far as to say that because she was already telling me more than she should have been telling me."

Maybe I'm a busybody and a nosey parker the way a lot of people say I am. Maybe it's just that I got more than the average share of curiosity. Maybe it's just that some little thing catches my attention, starts me wondering, and I can't let it rest until I explain it to my own satisfaction.

Anyway, Saturday morning I drive over to the building where Crank, Edgar, Asher, Somebody and Somebody have their offices on the off chance that Vollmer's secretary would be standing by catching any calls what might be coming in from clients who heard about his misfortune, but might not have his home number. I should say his wife's misfortune but for right now, until I know different, I'll call it his misfortune too.

The elevator takes me up to the thirtieth floor and opens out into this very large reception area with about two acres of deep-pile carpet, some suede leather couches with big glass-topped coffee tables along one wall, windows looking out on the city on another and doors leading to a corridor with offices on either side on the third. There's a Louis the Something desk in the middle of the ocean of rug but nobody's manning or womanning it. I go over and look at the small telephone exchange switch pad on one side of the desk. There's a light blinking on one of the stations. The nameplate next to it says F. VOLLMER.

When the light blinks out I press the button which rings the phone in Vollmer's office. Then I start walking across the floor and start down the corridor. In about a minute a blonde woman, dressed in slacks and a Mickey Mouse sweatshirt, pops out of one of the doors.

"Eeek!" she says.

"You don't have to eek," I says.

"Did you just buzz me from the desk?" she says.

"There was nobody there to announce me," I says.

"Because it's Saturday," she says.

"I took the chance that Frank—Mr. Vollmer—might be putting in some overtime."

"Not this Saturday. Who are you?"

"My name's Jimmy Flannery and I'm one of Mr. Vollmer's students over to his political science evening class at Chicago University."

"Haven't you heard that his wife's very ill in the hospital?"

"That's why I thought he might be working. Just to get his mind off his worries, you know. I do that whenever I got troubles. I try to find some work to do, something to occupy my mind."

"Well, Mr. Vollmer's at his wife's side," she says as though a dunce like me wouldn't know that it would be very unfeeling for anyone to seek forgetfulness in work instead of worrying about not being able to do anything for the person you care about.

"What did you want to see Mr. Vollmer about?" she asks, like she's expecting me to say nothing and beat a quick retreat.

"I wanted to thank him for doing a favor for a friend of mine."

"Couldn't that have waited until you saw him in class next time?" she asked, being very suspicious and showing it.

"Well, he wasn't in class, was he?"

She colors up a little at that.

"Of course not," she says, trying to make a quick recovery.

"I was in the neighborhood and I thought I'd thank him and maybe tell him how sorry I am about his wife."

That warms her up a little.

"Well . . . " I says.

"Yes?"

"I don't like to call somebody Miss or Miz or whatever."

"Oh. Jane. I'm Jane Carlisle, Mr. Vollmer's secretary, and I'm here for things just like this, anybody calling up or stopping by."

The phone rings inside the office and she pops back inside after telling me she'll tell Mr. Vollmer that I stopped in to offer my condolences the next time he stops by or calls in.

She's on the phone delivering the bad news and accepting condolences from the caller when I follow her inside. She looks up a little surprised, a little irritated. When she hangs up she asks, "Is there something else?" like she's getting more than a little fed up with me.

"It's none of my business but I was just wondering if Mr. Vollmer was here in the office when he got word that his wife was took—was taken, had been taken— ill."

"Are you a cop?" she asks, her jaw hardening.

"What would a cop be doing looking into Mrs. Vollmer's illness? Is there something unusual about Mrs. Vollmer's illness?"

I got her a little bit on the run. I asked a question that makes her think she's got to explain herself.

"I'd say it's always unusual when a healthy woman Mrs. Vollmer's age suddenly falls into a coma."

"You say she was healthy? Does that mean she wasn't on any medication?"

"If you're a police officer, I'd like you to show me some identification," she says.

"I ain't a police officer. I never said I was a police officer. I'm a concerned friend. I was just wondering if Frank had anybody around to give him some support when the phone call came in about his wife."

"I was here to give him support," she says.

"So he was right here when he got the call?"

"That's right."

"At around two o'clock in the afternoon?"

"Earlier than that. About an hour earlier than that."

"It must've hit him very hard."

"I'd say so. He sort of wandered out into my office, looked around as though he were in a daze, walked back inside, then came back again to tell me what he'd just been told by the housekeeper—"

"And hurried right on over to the hospital," I says, finishing it up for her.

"No. He went back into his office and didn't come out for two hours. He was very upset."

"Did he make any calls in that time?"

"Yes. I'm sure there were people he had to inform. Relatives. Friends."

"He ask you to dial the numbers?"

"He dialed them himself."

"So he talked to somebody for two hours."

"Not the whole two hours. His phone was in use only now and then."

I been asking questions so fast after I got her off balance with the first couple that she's been answering like she can't help herself. Also I got the feeling that something about that day when Vollmer got word about his wife's been bothering her, too, and it's a relief to put the burden over onto somebody else. But now she remembers who she is, Vollmer's secretary, and who I am, a stranger, and she picks up a pen and says, "What was your name again? Jimmy . . . ?"

"Flannery. Jimmy Flannery," I says, and she writes it down. "I'm going over to the hospital to see Frank," I says, "and see if maybe there's something I can do. But you can tell him that I stopped by if you want to."

"You're not going to . . . " she starts to say, but lets it lay there.

"Mention this conversation? No, I ain't."

That seems to settle her mind a little bit, but I can see she's still got a lot of doubts about a stranger who walks in with so many questions.

"So what time did he ask for the messenger?" I says, like it's something that just popped into my head.

"How do you know he called for a messenger?" she asks, her suspicions spilling over again.

"Because the paper the messenger delivered was the favor he did for my friend."

"The messenger picked up about three o'clock," she says.

"So, even though his wife had been rushed to the hospital, Frank took the time to finish a little thing like that and hand it over to a messenger. Ain't that just like Frank? Always thinking about others before hisself."

She looks at me like she thinks I'm trying to feed her some Irish honeycake but there's no way she can get mad on her boss's behalf about a compliment.

"I'll be going then," I says. "Thank you very much."

I can tell she's glad to see me go.

I stop in the doorway and I asks, "Your switchboard keep a log on outgoing calls?"

She's finally had enough of me. "That's none of your business, Mr. Flannery."

"Please, just call me Jimmy. Everybody does."

18

I meet Willy Dink over at the diner where he takes his messages. He hands me a plastic baggie with a couple of ounces of dried lion dung in it plus a pair of rubber surgical gloves.

"What's them for?" I'd asked him.

"Well, it ain't exactly winter, is it?" he says. "I think it'd look a little funny, you going around wearing a pair of regular gloves."

"Don't you think it's going to look just as funny, me going around wearing rubber gloves?"

"Make like they caught you doing the dishes."

"That ain't the right kind of rubber gloves."

"By the time they get to thinking about why you're wearing a pair of rubber gloves, you'll've already shook their hands and the lion smell'll already be all over them. Now, you just make sure you don't get any on yourself or Alfie won't have anything to do with you for a week."

I drive over to O'Meara's and take Alfie in the house

first, telling him to lay down in Billy's basket, Billy not being there.

"Where's Billy?" I asks Cora and Jake.

"He's with my mother, keeping her company," Cora says.

Jake looks at his watch. "You got about five minutes to do whatever you got to do. These people are right on time. You sure Alfie ain't going to trot over to them looking for a pet?"

"I got a feeling Alfie ain't going to like them any better than you do but just to be sure I'll go get ready. Now you be sure to give me a big introduction because I got to shake each and every hand."

I go put on the rubber gloves and then finger the dry dung in the baggie. It don't smell as bad as I thought it was going to smell. In fact it don't hardly smell at all, but then I ain't got a dog's nose who's probably got a better ancient memory for the smell of lion than humans do.

I ain't one to make my mind up about another person on first impressions. I mean some of the most innocent-looking people I ever met, like Chips Delvin, are the craftiest, some of the meanest-looking the sweetest, and the other way around.

But when I get a look at the late Mrs. Papadopolous's nieces and nephews I don't got—have—to have an affidavit to know that what we've got here is some very piggish people, the kind what applaud like mad when some crook gets up and says, "Greed is good," or some woman in a ten-thousand-dollar dress covering her bones says, "You can't be too thin or have too much money."

O'Meara's quick to meet them at the door so they can't all come piling in and maybe have one or two of them get around me, into the parlor and over to Alfie—playing like he's Billy—before I get to shake their hand.

"Hello, Mr. Papadopolous," he says to the first one what walks through the door, a big pushy type, with thinning hair and the blankest eyes I think I ever see on a person. "I'd like you to meet my teacher, Miss Cora Esper, and my friend, Committeeman James Flannery. Miss Esper, Mr. Flannery, I'd like to introduce George Papadopolous, Mrs. Papadopolous's nephew, her brother's son."

I don't know if he thinks practically giving Cora and me titles is going to impress them, but George's expression don't even flicker except he glances down briefly when he feels the texture of my hand, which in a rubber glove ain't quite natural.

O'Meara does the same for Martin Kalogeras, who is the late Mrs. Papadopolous's late sister's son, and Mrs. Theresa Bacos and Mrs. Thelma Argente, one of which is the daughter of her late husband's late brother and the other of which is her own late brother's daughter. All these details give me a chance to hold onto their hands for a minute to make sure the lion doo-doo really gets rubbed in.

The last one I shake hands with is Stanley Duskind, the lawyer. If George Papadopolous's eyes is blank, this one's eyes is like looking into a calculating machine. He's adding me up while we're holding hands, wondering if I'm another lawyer disguised as O'Meara's friend.

"Committeeman, did Mr. O'Meara say?" he asks.

"The Twenty-seventh."

"Old Delvin's ward?"

"That's right. Do you know Mr. Delvin?"

"I heard about him. Who hasn't heard about Chips Delvin? Passing of an era. A piece of Chicago history."

He's got this smile what flashes on and off like the strobe light on a camera. He gives me the old click-click which I think he thinks makes him a very charming person.

"You know Mr. O'Meara long?"

"I know him long enough to call him Pothole when I want to get his goat."

O'Meara looks at me funny, like he's surprised I'd know such a thing or even that I'd even know he had a nickname.

Duskind's smile goes click-click. "Do you know how he got that nickname?"

"I know, but I ain't telling," I says.

"A man of discretion," he says, and turns away from me. "Well, shall we make our inspection?"

"I'm curious about something," I says. "What's this inspection all about?"

"As the beneficiaries of the estate, my clients have a fiduciary interest in the maintenance of this property and the items held in trust and under guardianship."

"You're talking about Billy?"

"The dog. Yes, the dog."

"Thanks for helping me clear that up. For a minute there I didn't know what you was talking about. You see we don't call Billy the item."

"Well the orders of the court so designates the animal in question," Duskind says.

"Well, that's good to know," I says. "It tells me a lot about the temper of the court. But it still don't tell me if it spells out you got the right to come here inspecting the property or whatever anytime you decide you want to."

"You know a little about the law, do you, Mr. Flannery?"

"I pick up a little doing what I do."

"I could go through the trouble and expense of getting a court order," he says.

"I wouldn't ask you to do that. You put my friend through the trouble and expense of getting an order to keep you from torturing Billy—"

"Please," he says, raising a hand, asking me not to be so harsh in my description.

"—but O'Meara ain't the kind to get even if it means acting small. Besides, there's nothing to hide around here. You want to go in, take Billy's pulse, see how long the poor old man's got to live, nobody's going to mind. As long as you don't hurt him. As long as you don't stick a needle in him."

I figure I got everybody feeling nervous and maybe even a little bit guilty for doing what they're doing. Well, at least the nieces and Martin Kalogeras look a little uncomfortable. My trying to play a tune on their heartstrings ain't bothered George Papadopolous or Duskind one little bit.

Click-click goes Duskind. "Let's go in and have a look around, shall we?"

When we get to the kitchen one of the nieces,

Theresa Bacos, makes a little mew of concern when she sees Alfie laying there in Billy's bed, his head on his paws, bored brainless with it all, just hanging in until I give him the word that we can get the hell out of there.

Theresa hunkers down—I notice she ain't got a bad set of stilts—and reaches out the back of her hand to give Alfie a sniff, the way they tell you to do with dogs you don't know really well.

Alfie sits up like a bee stung him and backs off like she's threatening him with a gun.

"Billy, Billy, Billy," she coos.

Alfie gives her a little growl. It's bad enough she smells bad, but her calling him by another name is the final insult.

Martin Kalogeras gives this phony hearty laugh and says, "The dog doesn't like you, Tess."

"He may be getting old but he shows good sense," Thelma says, sticking in her two cents and demonstrating to anybody what's paying attention that these ladies don't get along too well.

Kalogeras tries to give Alfie a pat on the head, being a little bolder about it, sticking his hand right down there like the dog he thinks is Billy wouldn't dare growl at him.

Alfie's ears go back and he snaps at the offending hand which Kalogeras snatches back just in time, otherwise he could've lost a finger.

"That old dog's acting awfully spry," he says.

"You scare an animal and he'll find a way to fight back even if he's dying," Cora says very sweetly.

She looks so fresh and pretty Papadopolous and

Kalogeras ain't about to take exception to anything she says, and since Thelma and Theresa didn't like her at first sight, she ain't lost any ground there.

"Get out of the way, Martin. Let me have a look at that dog," George Papadopolous says in this voice.

Martin steps aside but you can see he don't like being ordered around by his cousin.

Papadopolous reaches out his left hand. Alfie gets ready to take a nip but then Papadopolous grabs him by the scruff of the neck with his right hand and starts to hunch closer for a better look.

"Hey," O'Meara says. "Get your hands off that dog before I bust your fingers."

Papadopolous lets go fast and backs away, Alfie sitting there trembling and glaring at him very indignantly.

"Are you threatening me, O'Meara?" Papadopolous says.

"That's right. You were inflicting an injury on a ward of the court which has been put in my care. You ask your lawyer; I ask you to cease and desist and you don't, then I got a legal right to use all appropriate force to protect and defend the creature what is my responsibility."

"Oooof," Papadopolous says, like O'Meara's punched him in the belly. He looks at Duskind, who's got this little smile on his face which tells me that he don't much like George Papadopolous either. He gives a little shrug like he's not about to argue the legalities right here in somebody's kitchen.

What we got here is a lot of people what don't like one another and are joined together only because of fi-

nancial considerations. Sometimes that can be a powerful glue and sometimes that can be otherwise.

"Would you like to look at the rest of the house?"
Cora asks like there ain't a bit of tension in the air.
"Watch your clothes. We've been painting, improving
the property, and some places are still wet."

19

I take a drive over to Illinois Masonic to pay my respects to Frank Vollmer and see if there's anything I
can do in his time of trouble. Also to have another
look at the pearlescent white Jaguar. I walk up and
down the lines of cars until I find it. I take down the
plate number and then I go into the hospital and ask
at reception for Mrs. Vollmer's room.

The receptionist asks me if I'm family and when I
tell her I ain't—I'm not—she tells me that only family
is allowed.

"Is her husband with her?" I asks.

"I wouldn't know that, sir."

"Maybe I could at least talk to somebody at the
nurses' station," I says. "I'd like to have a word with
Mr. Vollmer."

"Is it very important?"

"Well, compared to a wife what's in a coma, I'd say
no. But, on the other hand, it might give Frank—Mr.

Vollmer—a little comfort," I says, smiling this wistful smile I trot out for such occasions.

"Well, if you walk along this corridor and turn left you'll come to the nurses' station," she says. "But, if anybody asks, don't tell them I let you through."

I take the route she points out which takes me past a couple of public telephones on the wall with privacy booths around them. Vollmer's on the phone in one of them with his back to me.

I see the number of Mrs. Vollmer's room on one of the doors and I walk over and go inside. They got the shades drawn with just the night-light on.

Mrs. Vollmer is a very pretty woman lying there with her hair fanned out on the pillow and one of them plastic harnesses to deliver oxygen around her head and in her nose. And her eyes is closed as she breathes very gently.

I'm standing there looking down at her, wondering why a woman like her would want to take her life—if that's what she done—did—when she stirs a little and her eyes flutter open.

I know enough from talking to Mary to know that don't necessarily mean she's coming out of it but I grab the moment just in case and take her hand, so she'll have something—somebody—outside herself to connect with.

"Dolce?" she mumbles at me. At least that's what I think she says. I think maybe she said "Dolly" or "Dollin," but then she says it again. I'm pretty sure it's "Dolce." And then her eyes flutter closed again and she's back in a deep sleep again.

I let go her hand and walk back out into the corridor.

Vollmer's still on the phone. I stop about six feet back and stand there waiting for him to finish.

One minute he's laughing and the next minute he's hunched over the handset talking into it like he's trying hard to make a case for something to the person on the other end of the line.

Maybe he feels me looking at him like people do, because he tosses a glance my way over his shoulder and when he sees me suddenly gets red in the face and more than a little flustered. Which I think is something to think about since him being an attorney and standing up there teaching and all, you'd expect better control over hisself when confronted with minor surprises.

He says a quick good-bye, hangs up and turns to me with a smile and eyebrows that're asking me what I'm doing there.

"You visiting somebody?" he asks.

"Well, actually, I come to inquire about your wife and maybe see was you around."

"What for?"

"Well, to thank you for taking care of that little thing for that friend of mine, but mostly to see if there's anything I can do."

"That's very kind of you, Jimmy," he says.

"That's all right, Frank. This is a very tough world we live in and we got to help one another all we can. Is your wife doing better?"

"She's holding her own but I wouldn't say she was doing better."

"You know what happened?"

He stares into my eyes for a minute like he's wondering why he should discuss private family matters with a comparative stranger, no matter how well meaning, and I guess he sees something there that gives him confidence or maybe he just needs somebody to talk to, so he says, "I came home from school and found her unconscious."

"So you had to rush her to Emergency," I says.

"I called her doctor." He stands there for a minute just looking at me again. "I didn't realize how serious it was."

"Her being unconscious?"

"That's right. I thought she was just passed out."

"Uh," I says, which is a remark he can take any way he wants to take it; that I understand what he's getting at, that I don't understand and need more information or that I'm just sympathizing.

"Over the last year or so, I've often come home to find Joan passed out."

"I'm sorry. I didn't mean to—"

"That's all right."

"—intrude."

"That's all right. It's a wonder everybody in town doesn't know about it by now. She's had a few near accidents in public places, a couple of sly mentions in the gossip columns."

"I don't read that stuff," I says.

"I don't suppose you would, Jimmy. I can see that you're not the sort of man who'd have much interest in such things. Well, we—myself and her friends—were doing our best to keep it quiet."

"So you thought she was just drunk again?" I says.

"Until she failed to respond in spite of everything I tried to do."

I almost asked him what he tried to do, but that would've shut him up, a stranger questioning him that way, so I just stood there letting him talk it out the way he wanted to.

"I called the doctor," he says.

All of a sudden his face squeezes up like he's in pain and he turns away like he's going to cry and he don't want me to see. I put out my hand and pat him on the shoulder, telling him it's okay he wants to let go and relieve himself. He shudders and when he turns back to face me, he's composed hisself.

"If my delay causes some permanent damage or . . ." he don't say anything about her death but I know that's what he means ". . . I don't know if I'll ever be able to forgive myself."

"You done what you thought was best. A person can't do better than that."

"Thank you for saying that, Jimmy. Right this minute I'm not sure I really believe it, but it's a comfort to hear."

"There anything I can do?" I asks. "Anything at all?"

"You stopping by to see how Joan and I were doing means more than I can say," he tells me. "You're a good friend, Jimmy."

"Speaking of which, I'd like to tell you thanks again for what you did for O'Meara. I was over to his place and he told me how you sent that cease and desist petition over by messenger. I mean that was an awful nice thing to do seeing as how you had these heavy worries on your mind."

"It helps to keep your mind occupied."

"Amen to that," I says.

We shake hands and I go on my way wondering if what I was just part of—Vollmer revealing all that private stuff to me—might not've been a rehearsal for the story Vollmer intended to tell one and all and there was me being the tryout audience.

Thinking that I was a rat to be doing what I was about to do, if Vollmer had been telling me the truth about his wife's drinking and all, I found myself another public telephone in another part of the hospital and called a friend of mine down at Motor Vehicles who ran the number of the plate I'd taken off the pearlescent white Jag.

It's registered to a Miss Constance DeJohn at an address over by the Lincoln Park Zoo.

20

Lincoln Park West is a short boulevard with the park on one side and rows of very upmarket apartment houses on the other.

Miss DeJohn's apartment is on the eighth floor.

The elevator's paneled in rosewood and it's got a mirrored ceiling. Very posh, like they say.

It's about seven o'clock when I arrive at her door and ring the bell.

I hear heels click-clacking across marble floors.

When Mrs. DiBella opens the door she's already saying, "I thought we were going to be smart about this and—"

And she sees me and shuts up like I cut her throat.

I'm as surprised to see her as she is to see a stranger at her door.

"Yes?" she says like she's really saying, "Who the hell are you, what the hell do you want and how quick can you find yourself back to whatever gutter you crawled out of?"

"I'm looking for Gypsy Segal," I says.

"There's no gypsies here," she says with this little frown scratching a few lines on her forehead.

"Ah, Jesus, Manny give me the wrong directions again," I says, starting to turn away.

"Hold on a second, haven't I seen—" she starts to say, just as I hear the elevator open behind me down the hall. It gets her attention, too, and she turns her head to look. "Frank," she says.

I try to turn the other way, not knowing what to do with my face, though how I thought I was going to hide myself I don't know.

"Flannery," Vollmer says.

And almost in the same second, Mrs. DiBella finishes what she started to say. "—seen you somewhere before," she says. "At the funeral parlor."

"What are you doing here, Flannery?" Vollmer says, rushing up and getting into my face.

I back off two steps.

"Looking for you, Frank," I says. "After I left you at the hospital I thought of something else."

"What's that?" he says automatically, not giving a thought to what I said, just coming back at me because he don't know what's going on here.

She plucks at his sleeve.

"Connie, don't drag on me. What the hell are you talking about, Flannery?" he says, finally getting what I said and the improbability of it. "How would you know I was coming here?"

"Get inside here, Frank, for God's sake," Connie says.

He realizes that we're standing right out there in

the hall where the neighbors can hear if they happen to walk out into the hall or stick their ear to the door, so he lets hisself be pulled inside, reaching out to pull me inside after him.

Connie's recovered herself quicker than Vollmer.

"Please sit down, Mr. Flannery," she says. "Can I get you a drink?"

"I'll have a scotch on the rocks," Vollmer says.

"And you, Mr. Flannery?"

"A glass of ginger ale would be nice if you got it," I says.

"Please go into the living room," she says. "Make yourself comfortable."

We go into this very tasteful living room what looks like it come out of a decorator's showroom. There's a big picture window looking out on the city and Lincoln Park below.

"All right, then, how did you get here?" Vollmer says.

"I noticed the car you're driving now is a different color from the one you was driving the first time I saw you on the parking lot over to the University. It changed color right after you turned the class over to me that night and Pastorelli followed you out and got hisself killed. So tonight I got the number on the plate from the Jag you had parked in the hospital parking garage and here I am."

"From the Jaguar in the hospital garage? Do you think there's only one pearl-white Jaguar in Chicago?"

"Well, you take these little shots in the dark and sometimes they pay off," not pointing out what a silly defense he's handing me in view of the fact that he's here and I'm here and the white Jag is no doubt sitting downstairs at the curb. "Yours was the only one parked at Illinois Masonic tonight."

"You've got a nerve," he says.

Connie walks in with the refreshment on a silver tray and sets it down on a steel and limestone coffee table in front of this eight-foot couch covered in cream-colored linen.

"What's your game?" she asks.

"What do you want?" he asks.

"Hold it," I says.

"What's your price? How much?" Vollmer says, in this very aggressive, threatening way.

"Let's hear what Mr. Flannery has to say, Frank," Connie says. "He can't very well tell us what he wants if you keep barking at him."

Vollmer sits down in a chair that matches the couch and I sit down on the couch. Connie sits next to me. I got to admit I'm very conscious of her body being so close to me. She still looks naked, even in her jumpsuit.

"What I want is to find out what happened the Thursday night that Pastorelli got hisself killed."

Vollmer's trying to work his way through his options. Connie's quicker than him.

"Well, part of it's obvious, isn't it?"

"You mean the part about Frank here having a relationship with you, with Joseph DiBella's wife?"

"Can you figure out the rest of it?" Vollmer says.

"I don't think I can give you the details but I can give you the broad strokes," I says.

"Go ahead," he says, leaning forward like he's ready

to listen to some client's tale of woe and offer his advice for a fee.

"For some reason Mrs. DiBella, here, wanted to see you about something that couldn't wait. Maybe you'd been ducking her—"

He looks at her and smiles and she smiles back. I even expect them to reach out and hold hands, showing what lovebirds they are in front of a doubting stranger.

"—but maybe not. Anyway it was something that couldn't wait until the regular time you got together here in this little love nest. Like an hour or two after class?"

"Love nest," Vollmer says, like he's amused at something that sounds so old-fashioned.

"Or maybe it'd been sometime before you was together because DiBella was suspicious and had some of his people, including Vince Pastorelli, keeping an eye on you night and day. So you walked out of the class that Thursday night after Pastorelli fell asleep like he usually done—did. But Pastorelli woke up, found you gone, figured out where you went and hurried on out to get on your tail because if you managed to slip one over on him Joseph DiBella wouldn't be very glad about it."

"He's pretty good," Vollmer says, smiling at Connie.

"Have I got something wrong?"

"Joe didn't have any ideas about Frank and me," Connie says in a whispery voice.

"What then? He was having you watched, wasn't he?" I says.

"Sure he was," Vollmer says. "But it was business he was thinking about."

He waits for me to work it out.

"Which one of them you was going to hand the contracts out to?" I says.

He nods his head.

"Then how come Pastorelli knew where to go to find you?"

"Oh, come on, Flannery, don't disappoint me," Vollmer says.

"He just stumbled on the connection between us one day," Connie says. "We were meeting for lunch at the restaurant in the Chicago Institute. Who would've believed that Vinnie had a taste for Seurat's *Sunday in the Park*?"

Which is not the real title of that picture but I don't correct her.

"All perfectly innocent, we told him," Vollmer says. "We thought Vinnie bought it. We thought he was dumber than he really was."

"He must've followed me and found out I had this apartment that nobody, especially not Joe, knew about," Connie says. "It's the way things happen. You think you've got everything covered and then . . ." She don't—doesn't—finish the sentence because she knows she don't have to.

"So that Thursday night Pastorelli sees your Jaguar, the silver-gray one, parked outside this apartment house," I says to Vollmer, "and he waits for you until you come out and then he confronts you. Accuses you of cheating on Joseph with DiBella's wife. Maybe threatens to beat up on you. That's not a pleasant thought, so you run over him with the Jaguar."

"Trying to get away. Just trying to get away," Vollmer says. "I just panicked."

"You didn't mean to kill him," I says.

"Of course not. I'd never use violence. I'm a negotiator. I would've found Vinnie's price."

"Not likely," I says.

"I would've sold him a story," Vollmer says, and for a minute there I really think he could've. At least I think he thinks he could've.

"How many times you hit him with the car?" I says.

He stares at me and finally he says, "Just once. It was an accident. I was trying to get away."

I finish the ginger ale and stand up.

"What are you going to do now?" Connie asks.

"I don't know what I can do," I says.

"That's right. You take that to the police, who's going to believe it? How are you going to prove it?" Vollmer says. "It's just a story."

"There's people would believe it."

Fear flashes across Vollmer's face. I look at Connie, and she's gone dead white. Her lipstick makes her mouth a bloody slash. "You'd be as good as murdering us if you told Joe," she says.

"That I wouldn't do," I says. "But figure it out for yourself. Pastorelli's body's found in the park across the street. You think the DiBellas believe an old bone-breaker like Pastorelli was mugged? If there was enough of them, a gang out wilding that night might've taken him, but he would've left one or two laying beside him with bullets in their eyes. Joseph's got his people looking at this street, you can bet on that. You ain't as smart as you think you are, Frank. If I was you, I'd leave here the back way."

"I intend to," Vollmer says. "I was just bringing Connie's car back to her."

"The pearlescent white Jag you bought her?"

He gives me a little nod.

"So your Jag's out of the shop, then," I says.

"They did a great job. You ought to get your car painted at Devon Downs," Vollmer says.

"Too rich for my blood."

"I could just have them add the price to my invoice."

"You don't know me that well, Mr. Vollmer," I says.

21

It's Sunday again. Mary and me—I—and the baby go
over to my father's, her mother's, house for dinner.

Aunt Sada's there like always.

While the women are in the kitchen helping with
the dinner, I'm sitting in the parlor with Mike, Kathleen sleeping on my lap, gossiping.

"The way things keep changing, you can't keep up,"
I complain.

"There comes an age when you start thinking that."

"For God's sake, you make it sound like I'm over the
hill," I says.

"That's the way life is, a bunch of hills. You go up
one, you go down another, you hope that there's another hill to climb in front of you. When you got no
more hills to climb you got to hope you're on top of
one of them so you got the view."

Every once in a while Mike gets very philosophical.

"We're all addicts," he says. "Human beings is all
addicts."

"For what?"

"New beginnings. Some more than others, but we're all addicted to new beginnings."

"Sometimes I'd just as soon there wasn't any more new beginnings. Sometimes I wish things would just stay the same for ever and ever."

"Things stayed the same for ever and ever, that little angel on your lap wouldn't be there. The sound of the women out in the kitchen wouldn't be there. We'd be a couple of old bachelors, you and me."

"You happen to know what happened to Joseph Di-Bella's first wife?"

"What makes you ask?"

"I don't know, we're talking about wives and kiddies and all of a sudden it pops into my mind."

"Which means you've been giving a lot of thought to this gangster's domestic arrangements?"

"So, do you happen to know?"

"The DiBellas ain't exactly what you'd call intimates of mine."

"But naturally they're talked about here and there, in the various places where you kill an hour or two now and then."

"Joseph's wife died about five years ago, if I remember it right. After that he had the usual collection of bimbos on his arm until one of them got her hooks in."

"This Connie."

"A better class of bimbo, I've been told. An old man's comfort."

"Joseph ain't that old. He ain't too old to be in the

struggle for his brother's action now that Carmine's gone home."

"Also like an old man's spur, you know what I mean. I think, if it wasn't for Connie, Joseph would just as soon one of his nephews took over the business. He's got all the money he could ever spend."

"But not all the money she could ever spend?"

"Well, if it's money she wants. I wouldn't know. If I was you I wouldn't keep on pursuing this interest."

"You told me once and I ain't exactly pursuing it," I says, "but just looking around casually. It looks like my classmate, Vincent Pastorelli, was done with a deadly vehicle and I got every reason to believe the vehicle belongs to Frank Vollmer."

"What?" Mike says, sitting up a little straighter. "What the hell would Vollmer be doing killing somebody . . . anybody?"

"To keep the news that he was playing around with DiBella's wife from the husband."

"You telling me that Vollmer was dumb enough to go after Joseph DiBella's young wife? Forget he loves her if he loves her. Forget he wants her if he wants her. She's a prize for an old man like DiBella. You steal his prize it's a point of honor and you ain't long for this world."

"Which is part of what's got me wondering. It looks to me like Pastorelli was sitting in on Vollmer's class just to keep an eye on him. To *let* Vollmer know that he was keeping an eye on him. Which says to me that DiBella already had reason to be suspicious. Which makes me wonder why Vollmer took the chance, leaving the class and going over to see Connie DiBella in this flat she kept—and maybe Vollmer paid for—over on Lincoln Park West, with Pastorelli sitting right there in class."

"Asleep. Didn't you tell me Pastorelli always fell asleep?"

"What kind of guarantee did Vollmer have that Pastorelli would stay asleep? Why did he take the chance?"

"I ain't got a clue. You got any ideas?"

"The only idea I got is that Connie DiBella handed Vollmer some kind of ultimatum. Got him over there that night because she wanted DiBella to know and wanted Vollmer to know that DiBella knew that there was a little hanky-panky going on."

"What the hell for? Why's she want to risk a bullet in the eye? What you're saying is crazy. Why would she do a thing like that?"

"To give DiBella a lever. You were talking about an old man with a young wife. You were talking about money and somebody who's got all the money he can ever use. You talk about honor and a man who makes up his own rules about honor when it suits his purpose. For instance that old wheeze about honor among thieves is donkey dust and everybody knows it. But there's one thing we ain't talked about which could give us motive, reason and explanation."

"What's that?"

"Power. How much you want to bet?"

"Bet on what?"

"How much do you want to bet that any day now it's in the news that the Municipal Pier, Canal, Garages, Public Curbs and Expansion Agency gives the new contracts for managing the parking garages, lots and meters to a company what is fronted by somebody legitimate but is owned by Joseph DiBella? That's the bet."

22

The next night—which is Monday night rolling around again—Janet Canarias stops in.

"Well, it happened just like we expected it was going to happen," she says. "They've privatized parking garages, lots and meters."

"Just like *you* said it was going to happen," I says. "I can't take no credit for seeing that one coming. So, what do you think? You think it's such an awful thing that garages, lots and meters goes private. City, county and state services are going private all over the place. I read about a Japanese company here, a German company there, taking on the contract for prison management."

"There's something a little ironical there, wouldn't you say, Jimmy?"

"I was too young for the Second World War—"

"And so was I."

"—but my old man is all the time saying what a funny thing it is that the two countries we had to go to war with and beat are the ones we spent billions on reconstructing and defending and now they're beating the socks off us every which way you can name."

"Perhaps what we have here is something very similar," she says.

"How's that?"

"The criminal syndicates, the gangs from the thirties and the forties, the Mafia who've grown up and grown older, first they muscled into businesses, commercial laundries, magazine distribution, trash pickup, the unions, the dockworkers and truckers, they went legitimate."

"Cleaned their fingernails, hired lawyers and accountants—"

"Fashion experts to color-coordinate their suits and ties."

"Started bidding contracts just like any other company is what you're saying."

"That's right, but still knowing how to manipulate. Intimidate. People don't throw away tried and true methods of conducting business just because they retire their baseball bats and sawed-off shotguns."

"What've you heard that I ain't heard?" I says, knowing that all this talk about criminals sticking their snouts in the barrel ain't just speculation.

"The contracts have already been given out. It was a done deal before they announced the privatization. Oh, they'll go through the bidding process. They'll put on the public show. But it's already a done deal."

"You know that for certain?"

"As certain as I can be about anything in a system where not only doesn't the left hand always know what the right hand's doing, but the pinkie finger can't even trust its own thumb. So . . ."

"So, what?"

"What I don't know and haven't yet been able to find out is the name of the person who was awarded the contracts and the name of the company fronting."

"So, it's still possible that whoever got the contracts could be legitimate?" I says.

One of her eyebrows pops up like a flag, asking me was I born yesterday or did I just fall off a turnip truck.

"You want me to ask around?"

"I want you to go to a primary source."

That bothers me a little. This is the kind of favor where you could end up owing a favor to someone you wouldn't really want to owe a favor to. She sees I'm hesitating.

"I'm not asking you to do something you don't think you can conveniently do."

"Whatever you ask me to do, I'll do. I'm just figuring out how I should go about it. There's a long way and there's a short way."

"What's the difference?"

"The short way could cost me more."

"I wouldn't want you to have to pay more than it's worth, but the quicker I know what's what the sooner I can throw a wrench into the machinery."

Here's this woman who beat the odds against sex and race, ready to put herself on the line and challenge the most important people in the city.

"I want some of that revenue for my minority people," she says, like she's reading my mind. "I've got young blacks and Hispanics with business degrees who can't get a decent entry level job and can't get a bank loan to start their own businesses who can do as well or better than any marginal operator a generation away from bone-breaking."

"Maybe not even that far," I says.

"If there's a danger."

"If you ain't afraid, how can I be afraid?" I says.

"Because you're a man and I'm a woman?"

"No, because you and me, we're both junkyard dogs when it comes to fighting for what we think is right. Don't you worry. I'll get the information you want. I'll give you the way to cut these suckers off at the pass before they announce the deal they already made."

23

I figure to go to the horse's mouth, right to Frank Vollmer, chairman of the Municipal Pier, Canal, Garages, Public Curbs and Expansion Agency, the man who was the man whose name would be on the contracts along with the name of the mayor's administrative assistant and maybe the mayor, hisself.

But I can't find him. He ain't at the hospital where his wife's still going in and out of the coma. He ain't at home where his maid tells me she ain't seen him in three days. He ain't at the office, where his secretary not only lets me look into his office to prove to me she ain't handing me a dodge but actually asks my help; if I find out where he is she'd sure be glad if I'd let her know. He ain't even over to the apartment on Lincoln Park West which him—he—and Connie DiBella used for a playground.

She ain't there either. I figure she's staying home nights.

I wanted to go to Frank Vollmer because that was

the shortest way and with what I know about him and Connie I figure I can twist his arm and get the truth.

There's the long way, using the old wisdom about being able to reach practically any person or get the answer to practically any question with three introductions or phone calls, and then there's a medium way, which also could cost me.

Vito Vellitri, the warlord of the Twenty-fifth, has been a man of respect and power since I was a pup, maybe before I was nothing but a gleam in my old man's eye, like the saying goes.

It's hard to say is he part of the Mob, ain't he part of the Mob. I'd bet on not. I mean not in any formal way. He's connected—how could he not be connected—but I think he stays aloof from any exchange of cash and out of the ordinary influence because he's more valuable to everybody as a man of honor. Sort of like how a prince of the church can deal evenhandedly with one and all as long as he keeps his skirts clean.

I've met Vellitri a hundred times at this or that political function. I seen—saw—him a couple of times over to Delvin's house. Whenever I saw him at his office or his home I been brought there by these two panthers, Ginger and Finks.

When I took on the job of committeeman in the Twenty-seventh, Delvin asks me over to his house. Vellitri was already there. He congratulates me on my new position and treats me like an equal, even though we've had our differences in the past when threats passed between us. He hands me his card with his private number and tells me to call him anytime I need his help.

This is not the shortest, but it also ain't the longest way to get the information that Janet Canarias wants.

I make the call and Vellitri hisself picks up. I tell him I'd like an appointment.

"Is there an urgency?" he asks.

"The sooner the better, if it's convenient," I says.

"Where are you?"

"At my house."

"Wait down front. I'll send Ginger and Finks. Ten minutes."

I don't know where Ginger and Finks was hanging out, but ten minutes they're there.

It's very funny riding in the back of the big black limo when I ain't under restraint or constraint or whatever. They think it's funny too.

"You know what, Ginger?" Finks says to Ginger who's driving.

"What?" Ginger says.

"It ain't the same."

"What ain't the same?"

"It don't feel the same driving Flannery, here, over to see the boss the way we're doing."

"What're you talking about? We done it plenty of times before."

"But we always had to come and get him. He wasn't coming willingly."

Ginger thinks about that. After a while he says, "I know what you mean."

They show me into Vellitri's library. He's sitting behind his big desk as usual, looking smaller than I remember, sitting there in this big plush chair with the carved wooden back, reminding me more than ever of some really old prince of the church, his thin, small, white hands laying there on the arms of the chair like a couple of hands carved out of ivory.

We go through the usual refreshment ritual and he sends Ginger and Finks off to get us both a couple of espressos.

They're back inside of three minutes with the cups, sugar bowl, lemon twists and silver pot on a tray. Vellitri sends them away and pours hisself.

Finally he says, "How can I be of service?"

"You know a lawyer by the name of Frank Vollmer."

It ain't quite a question because I know that Vellitri would know Vollmer, but he nods his head and says, "A partner in the firm of Crank, Edgar, Asher, McGargle and Vollmer."

"That's the man."

"Also the chairman of the board of the Municipal Pier, Canal, Garages, Public Curbs and Expansion Agency," Vellitri goes on.

"I don't have to ask do you know the DiBellas."

Right after I say it, I realize that's the kind of remark a man like Vellitri could take the wrong way since he's very sensitive about any suggestion that he's got contacts with the Mob even though, one way you look at it, the Mob ain't the Mob like it used to be the Mob, just like the Machine ain't the Machine like it used to be the Machine. But he don't take offense, he just smiles a little smile like he's amused at my brashness and nods his head.

"Carmine DiBella was a school chum of mine."

"I thought Mr. DiBella was raised in Sicily and didn't get to this country until he was eighteen, nineteen."

"He was and he didn't. I'm talking night school."

Vellitri speaks English with practically no accent as good as me so it never enters my mind that he was a refugee and had to learn the language after he was practically a grown man.

"How come he didn't name his heir when he went back to the old country?"

"He never consulted me on business matters as a rule. You understand, we were working different sides of the street and it wouldn't have looked right."

"Still, in friendly conversation, he might have mentioned it?"

"He mentioned it." He takes a tiny sip from the little white porcelain cup with the gold rim around it. By this time I know Vellitri good enough to know this is one of his stalls, one of the ways he gives hisself time to think something over.

He sets down the cup on the saucer. It don't even make a click.

He taps hisself on the side of his head and then on his chest on the left side.

"A disagreement between the head and the heart."

He's delivered the idea. I wait for the explanation.

"He loves his brother's son the most. The brother resisted the riches and temptations of the family business. Having no sons of his own, Carmine covets his brother's son, the prize his brother tries to deny him. So that's where his favor would go. How can it be any other way?" he goes on.

"Flesh of my flesh . . ." I murmurs, getting caught up in the scholarly atmosphere he's creating.

"The power over the nephew denied him."

He gives me one of those nods which is also like a blessing. "This nephew is easily seduced. But he's not very smart. Under Carmine's instruction all he becomes is a brute, a man who will always use the fist instead of the negotiation, not the best man to become the CEO of a prosperous and widespread enterprise. He never acquired the polish which came naturally to his uncle and teacher.

"So Carmine turns his eyes to his sister's son who doesn't bear the DiBella name but has all the smoothness and polish and intelligence anyone could require. He admires and respects his nephew, Bruno Falduto, the son of his sister who the women call sweet for more reasons than one. He admires and respects Bruno's choice of a wife even more."

"Angelina Donato."

Vellitri nods. "Carmine, the patriarch, has invited Bruno and his fiancée to have the wedding ceremony in Sicily when the time comes. He intends to charter two airplanes big enough to accommodate eight hundred wedding guests who are to be flown from here to there at his expense. Also they will be housed and fêted at his expense during a celebration that will last three days."

"An unusual honor," I says.

"A mark of his high regard. If he were to choose his successor only with his head, Bruno Falduto would be the man."

"And his brother, Joseph?"

"Here the head and the heart are in serious conflict. Carmine loves Joseph, his only surviving brother. If the truth were known he would prefer Joseph to come to Sicily and share in his retirement. But he understands. The younger brother feels himself too long in the shadow of the older all these years while being the faithful lieutenant and advisor. Now Joseph would like his hour in the sun. But he has done a foolish thing according to Carmine's view of things."

"He married Connie."

Vellitri's eyebrows comment on my familiarity.

"The present Mrs. DiBella," I quickly add, thinking that I'd like to have talented eyebrows like Vellitri and other people of my acquaintance have. When I've tried doing it in the mirror, I just look like a startled monkey, if you ever happened to see a startled monkey.

"That's right. Carmine feels that for a man Joseph's age to take on a second wife the age of Constance is not the act of a prudent man."

"Do you mean Carmine has doubts about her fidelity and loyalty?"

His eyelids drop a fraction, which I know from experience means he's pulling down the shades, ready to conceal information he's received in confidence. Still, I can't be sure if he's gotten wind of the games Connie DiBella's playing with Frank Vollmer over in that fancy playpen on Lincoln Park West, so I don't know if it would be very smart for me to tell him I already know about it. It's one of those delicate situations you got to get around without coming right out with naming it.

"A sensible man recognizes the danger," he says.

Which is one of them double entries they talk about. You know what I mean? If I let him know I know about Vollmer and Connie playing pitty-pat, then he's honor bound to mention it to Joseph DiBella that they ain't been very discreet, the word obviously getting out, and that might not sit very well with Di-Bella who could shun Vellitri. Like shooting the messenger who brings bad news. So he's warning me off with a little more than a raise of the eyebrows.

"What plan does Carmine DiBella have to solve this problem of who's going to succeed him?" I asks.

"Carmine DiBella's organization, just like governments, can run itself for quite some time without someone at the reins. There are advisors, counselors, attorneys, accountants, managers. . . . You understand. But a decision will have to be made sooner or later. If the problem were mine . . ." He don't say that he knows what Carmine intends to do or is already doing. ". . . I would set a task that would test the candidates without concentrating on any one quality of intelligence or character."

"For instance?"

"A major acquisition of property or contract that would add greatly to revenue or influence."

I can't think of anything that would add revenue and influence quicker to any organization or business than the contract for the city parking garages, lots and meters.

The Municipal Pier, Canal, Garages, Public Curbs and Expansion Agency has been named as the agency to put out the bids and award the contracts.

Frank Vollmer, as the chairman of said agency, is going to have a lot to say who gets the business.

Frank Vollmer's having a dance with Connie Di-Bella, old Joseph DiBella's young wife.

Frank Vollmer's wife is in a coma over to Illinois Masonic.

Frank Vollmer is also missing but nobody's made any noise about it yet.

I'm at the end of what I can safely get from Vellitri, without stepping over the line, unless I can get one more thing from him off the cuff. That is if he knows the one more thing.

I drink the last of my espresso and stand up. He leans forward, like he's going to be polite and stand up too, but I wave him back and shake his hand when he settles down.

"Thank you, Mr. Vellitri," I says.

"Vito," he says. "Remember I asked you call me Vito."

Gave me permission, he means.

"Thank you, Vito," I says and walk to the door.

I stop with my hand on the handle and I says very casually, "If you was one of the contenders in Carmine DiBella's little contest and you wanted to influence a man like, say, Frank Vollmer over the matter of giving out some city contracts, how would you go about persuading him?"

"Specifically Frank Vollmer?"

"Specifically Frank Vollmer."

"If I were Anthony DiBella I would first try to buy him and then would threaten him and his loved ones with bodily harm."

I turn the knob and crack the door.

"If I were Bruno Falduto, I would offer money in large amounts."

I open the door halfway.

"If I were Joseph DiBella, and had suspicions that my relationship with Frank Vollmer was not a financial one alone, I would have a long conversation with him and explain the consequences of his behavior and what he must do to retrieve his honor and return my own."

I was out the door and it was like Vellitri never answered my last question, he'd only been talking to hisself.

24

I need an ear. Usually I think things out loud with Mary but this is a matter my involvement in which could worry her. Ditto my father. The ear I can turn to whenever I want to examine the benefits and draw-backs, the upside and the downside, without concern-ing myself is he worried about me so he can't give me a really objective evaluation, is Delvin.

So, like I been doing for years, I go over there on the El and walk through the old neighborhood and up the steps of the old house and ring the bell which Mrs. Thimble answers.

Even though she's been Delvin's housekeeper for some time now, I still can't get used to her answering the door, even though she scolds me over this and that just like old Mrs. Banjo—may she rest in peace—used to do.

But this time she don't scold me about letting in the cold air if it's winter, tracking in mud if it's spring or fall or letting in the hot air if it's summer. Her eyes are red so I can tell she's been crying.

"Is this a bad time to drop in, Mrs. Thimble?" I asks.

"When you get to be a certain age, no time is a good time to drop in, all the time is a bad time to drop in, but any time is better than no time because it can be the last time," she says as I slip inside into the dark hallway with all the brown pictures of ghosts from the past lining the walls.

There's the smell of a sickroom in the house which I never noticed so strong before, although Delvin's been threatening to die of one disease or another for as long as I can remember.

"Will you be wanting anything?" Mrs. Thimble asks.

"Give the man a toddy, for God's sake," Delvin's voice calls from the parlor. It hardly sounds like him, it's so weak and thready.

I walk into the living room with its overstuffed furniture, crocheted antimacassars, potted palms and lace curtains. They've brought the single bed out of the spare bedroom in here into the bay with the three windows. Even though it's a single, with its heavy mahogany footboard and headboard it crowds the room.

There's a side table covered with a cloth next to the bed. A whole bunch of bottles and glasses is—are—sitting on it, proving how sick he is to anyone who wants to count.

Delvin, in a clean flannel nightshirt with—swear to God—a shawl around his shoulders is laying there propped up on a couple of big pillows.

There's a doctor with him, standing there with this smile on his face like Delvin just told him a joke or regaled him with a story from the good old/bad old days. He's only a youngster.

I hear myself think that and it comes as a shock. It ain't often at my age that I bump into somebody in authority younger than me. It's something to think about.

"Is Mrs. Thimble off getting you a little something against the chill?" Delvin says, holding out a trembling hand.

"What chill? It's a lovely fine spring day," I says, in that hearty way of speaking you find yourself doing when you're around somebody who's sick, like talking louder than ordinary'll cheer them up. "Besides, you know I don't drink alcoholic beverages."

"For God's sake, have a little mercy, Jimmy. Don't shout. I ain't gone deaf, no matter what Mrs. Thimble might think."

"How do you do," the doctor says, sticking out his hand. "I'm Dr. Brian Toole without an O."

"Jim Flannery," I says, shaking his hand.

"Are you a relation?" Toole asks.

"I'm the boy's godfather," Delvin says, which is probably the most affectionate thing Delvin ever said about me in my presence.

"Ahhhh," Toole says.

Mrs. Thimble comes in then with a couple of fingers of whiskey in a glass. She hands it to me and says, "There's fresh water in the carafe on the side table if you should want it."

"Let me have your hand, son," Delvin says.

I take a step closer, reaching for his hand with my free hand, which he brushes aside as he goes for the glass in my other hand with hardly a tremor in his.

Toole plucks the glass from my hand as neat as a frog flicks a fly off a leaf, downs it in one go and puts the empty glass on the table as Delvin looks on in horror.

"Very thoughtful of you. It's not often nowadays that the doctor is offered a little refreshment when making a house call," he says.

"And not often nowadays that you make them," Delvin says.

"Mr. Delvin, you're at a crossroads—"

"Don't I know it?" Delvin says.

"—and I'm here to tell you in front of your godson—who may have some influence over you—that you must restrict your diet, refrain from alcohol, stop your smoking and get out there for some light exercise in God's good fresh air or you'll not be long for this world."

He snaps his bag—which was laying on the foot of the bed—shut, shakes my hand again, squeezes Delvin's wrist and leaves the room. We can hear Mrs. Thimble scurrying to be there to open the front door, her being from the generation that honored doctors just a little less than priests.

Delvin relaxes back against the pillows as though he no longer has to put up a brave front with the doctor gone and Mrs. Thimble out of the room, which pleases me in a funny kind of way, like it means he really does trust me and like me enough to let his hair down around me.

"Do I look like a fool to you, Jimmy?" he asks.

"I don't think I ever met a smarter, shrewder man in my whole life," I says, "not even counting out my own father."

"Then why do I go through these games tricking my own housekeeper, my doctor, even my friends, out of a little toddy now and then?"

"Because I think you like the game better than you like the whiskey," I says, pulling up a straight-backed chair.

He grins and for a minute there he's the age he was when I first met him, fifty, maybe fifty-five, when he was at his peak.

"Put up the shade and open the window a bit before you sit down, will you, Jimmy?"

"I thought you felt a chill."

He throws off the shawl. "It's like you say, Jimmy, a nice, warm, soft spring day. Let's get a little of it into this room, which must stink to high heaven of old bones."

I push the curtains aside and let the green roller shade up. I open the window from the top and bottom. The smell of flowers and grass comes into the room. I turn around and see Delvin laying there with his eyes closed, this smile on his face, and tears come up to my eyes because, in that second, I know he ain't going to be around very long. Not very long at all. When I sit down he turns his head and opens his eyes, still smiling.

"So you still think I'm a pretty shrewd fella?" he says.

"That's why I'm here."

"You got a problem?"

"I got a story that's at a turning. I told you some of it—maybe most of it—but there's some new developments and I don't know if I got a next step or should I take another step."

He settles back. "Tell me," he says, and I can practically see his brain opening up to collect whatever information I got to give him.

I refresh his memory about the first time I mentioned Frank Vollmer teaching class and Vincent Pastorelli keeping an eye on him and then getting knocked over and killed by an automobile which I'm almost dead certain is Vollmer's Jaguar.

I tell him about meeting Carmine DiBella's brother, Joseph, and his nephews, Anthony DiBella and Bruno Falduto. Also Anthony's wife, Gina, Bruno's bride-to-be, Angelina Donato, and finally Joseph's young wife, Connie.

I tell him how I meet her once over to the funeral home and once in the little love nest she's got set up with Frank Vollmer.

Delvin's eyebrows shoot up when I tell him that.

He already knows about Mrs. Vollmer being in the hospital.

I tell him about Frank Vollmer maybe going missing.

I tell him about my meeting with Vellitri and Delvin's eyebrows go popping up again. I don't think he likes that I went and consulted with Vellitri before coming to him in spite of the fact that considering Vellitri's connections it would be only natural for me to touch base with him.

When I'm finished he lays there staring out the window for a long time.

"So you got four basic questions here," he finally says. "One, you got to find out who knew what when about these city services going private and how many more are earmarked to do the same. Two, you got to figure out if Joseph's new wife, this Connie DiBella's, mother raised any stupid children. Three, you got to find out if Vollmer's missing or just in hiding, which maybe could be the next to toughest thing to find out."

"What's the toughest?"

"It ain't the most important, but it could be the toughest. It maybe could tell you a lot if you could find out who told Mrs. Vollmer that her husband was having a dance with another woman."

He reaches out a big hand and takes my wrist. His fingers go around it, no trouble, and when he squeezes down a little I can feel he's still got plenty of power left in him.

"James," he says, which I figure means he's about to say something very serious or maybe even very sentimental. "James."

"Yes sir?"

"Would it be against your principles to ask Mrs. Thimble if you might have another small toddy for yourself? For God's sake, lad, I'm ninety weary years old and it ain't like I've been a roaring drunk anytime in my life. What does a doctor as young as Toole know about it, with all his fancy medicines and injections? I remember old Doctor Mulligan. He always said a little tot of whiskey was good for the heart. And even if it ain't, it'll make an old man's heart glad."

What could I do? The man's got a tongue of liquid silver. I go out to the kitchen and make the request.

Mrs. Thimble sighs, smiles and pours two fingers into my glass.

"It's the constant struggle keeps us alive," she says. "A man's got to have his small triumphs."

I take the whiskey back to Delvin but he's asleep, the sunlight coming through the window warming him and, I pray, bringing him dreams of youth.

25

All of a sudden I'm hungry to be with my wife and baby.

So, I take a pass on doing jumping jacks and duck waddles over to the Paradise Health Club run by Shimmy Dugan and his girlfriend/boyfriend, Princess Grace. I think it's more important that I spend some time with Mary and Kathleen than I should sweat a bucket and lose maybe another ounce. Besides, I'm down to what you might call my fighting weight, only four or five pounds heavier than I was when I was twenty-five or -six.

Mary's very glad to hear that I'm staying home after supper, so I can tell she's been as lonely for me as I been for her, even though she's the one who kept me at the exercise for good reason.

I start helping with the dishes but she says, "No, you take Kathleen into the parlor and play with her. She hardly ever sees you."

I put a baby quilt on the floor and after making sure

there ain't no—any—drafts down there I put her down there on her back and lean over her, making eye connection with her, which is what mothers do from almost the first minute they touch their babies.

I read about how if a human being or a cat or practically any other living thing is there when a duckling hatches out, the little bird'll think the human being or the cat or whatever is its mother. They call it imprinting.

With human babies there's more to it than that, I'm sure. But the thing is, there's got to be this interaction, this give and take, between the grown-up and the baby, which is like a tune they're dancing to. I mean mothers do it because it's in their nature. I ain't so sure about men. I got a feeling that they got to learn to be parents even if being a father wasn't all that difficult.

So me and Kathleen makes eyes at each other, and I poke her very gentle with my finger and she grabs ahold, and I smile and she smiles. And we have like this conversation of silly noises. We get to know one another a little better.

After a while Mary comes in and sits down on the floor with us. She puts her arm around my shoulders. She says, "I bet if I gave her her bottle she'd settle down and go right off to sleep."

Which is what we do and then we go to bed ourselves which feels a little sinful, it still being light out.

Irish Catholics—even though I don't follow the faith—got all sorts of ways of feeling a little bit guilty about feeling too good. Mary don't have that problem.

*   *   *

We're laying there holding one another. Then we let go and lay on our backs with our bodies still touching along the side, still holding hands. Then we need to cool off a little and we move apart. That's the way it happens. We become separate people and all sorts of thoughts come crowding in.

"Would it be all right if I made a phone call?" I asks.

Mary laughs like I said something really funny. She rolls over on her belly, reaching out a hand to pat my chest.

"I won't think you're an insensitive brute if you do," she says.

I pick up the phone on the bedside table, which we had put there just a couple of months ago so one of us wouldn't have to get out of bed to answer the wall phone in the kitchen, the only phone we had for a long time.

I dial Janet Canarias's home number but get her machine. I don't leave a message but call the storefront office, the one she lets me use on Monday nights, and she's there.

"You still working?" I says the minute she says "Hello, Alderwoman Canarias's office," because I recognize her voice right away.

"Why, what time is it?" she asks, recognizing my voice too.

I look at the bedside clock.

"Seven o'clock," I says.

"Middle of the afternoon," she says.

"You work too hard and too long."

"You and me, Jimmy."

"Question?"

"Go ahead."

"You were the first one to bring up the possibility that there was a little game going about making certain city services private."

"And I was right, wasn't I?"

"I ain't saying you ain't—haven't—got a great gift of prophecy, but I'm just wondering if you didn't have a little advance information on that situation."

"You won't let me have any fun, will you, Flannery?" she says. "Okay, I didn't see the possibility in some tea leaves or dream it in a dream. I knew how and when it was going to happen weeks before I brought the subject up with you."

"Who told you, you don't mind my asking?"

"I can't give away a source, Jimmy. It was told in confidence."

"Do you think a lot more people than just you was—were—told in confidence?"

"Without a doubt, but my word was given to this individual and, no matter how many others this individual informed, that has to be my only concern."

"I agree. It ain't—isn't—important anyway. I think we can take it as a given that somebody spills the beans to one source, they spill them to many."

"And I thought I was special," Janet says, laughing about it.

"Well, thanks for your ear. Now go home and live a life," I says.

"Are you living a life?" she asks, the laughter still in her voice, with a little something extra. "I mean at the moment?"

"Janet wants to know if I'm living a life?" I says to Mary, wondering how come it is women can read things in a man's voice what a man can't read in a woman's voice. It gives them an edge.

Mary takes the phone from my hand and says, "Janet? He's living a life, you can bet on it."

I take back the phone. When Janet stops laughing this time I says, "Well, thanks again," and she says, "Just a second, Jimmy."

"Yes?"

"I notice you're still correcting yourself all the time."

"I'm practicing what I'm learning in night school."

"Oh," she says, "I'm not sure I like it. It *ain't* the Jimmy Flannery I know and love."

"What are you smiling about?" Mary asks.

"Janet just tells me that she don't—doesn't—like the way I'm talking lately."

"How's that?"

"All the time correcting my own grammar. She says it *ain't* me."

Mary thinks about that only a minute, then she kisses me on the shoulder and says, "She could be right."

So I got the answer to the first question Delvin tells me to think about. If Janet Canarias got the word far in advance of the action, that means other people, maybe not a lot but some, has got the word, too.

The answer to the second question, did Connie Di-Bella's mother raise any stupid children, is something

I got to puzzle out. I think I know what he means but I ain't exactly positive.

"Now you're frowning," Mary says.

I tell her the circumstances, finding Connie DiBella in a love nest with Frank Vollmer after meeting her at Vinnie Pastorelli's laying-out, and I tell her what Delvin said about that.

"There are two things you'll have to find out," Mary says. "One. How long has she been Mrs. DiBella? Who's paying for what you call the love nest? It could be her old apartment that she doesn't want to give up completely just yet."

"And Frank Vollmer walking through the door the way he done?"

"He didn't walk through the door. The way you tell the story you were standing at the door when he walked out of the elevator."

"So?"

"So he's a lawyer, isn't he? He might have been coming to see Connie DiBella about any number of things that had nothing to do with hanky-panky."

26

The first thing I do the next morning is I go over to the Hall of Records and look up the marriage certificate of one Joseph Annuncio DiBella, widower, and one Constance Aurelia DeJohn, spinster. They've been married less than a year which tells me that she had great expectations and the old man was a mighty disappointment on the honeymoon—which I doubt very strongly was what Connie DeJohn was looking for marrying a man his age—or the thing she had going with Vollmer was of longer standing than I figured at first or she likes to live right up there on the edge.

Cheating on a Mob boss, maybe the man who's going to be the boss of bosses now that his older brother is retired, sounds like asking for it no matter how you look at it.

Then I go over to the apartment house where she has the apartment and check on the notice by the mailboxes that the building is owned by Fenster Real Estate Management on State Street.

Ten minutes there, while I pretend to be a possible tenant if an apartment ever comes up vacant, tells me what I want to know.

"Do you mind telling me what attracted you to our building?" a lady by the name of Sue Bow asks me.

"Well, first of all the park. I like the idea of living across the street from a park, you know what I mean? Also I have a friend lives in the building."

She's nodding her head with a pleased smile on her face while I'm talking. Now she says, "Oh?"

"Ms. DeJohn."

The smile stays but now she looks like she's trying to place the name. She goes to a tickle file and does a quick, efficient search. Now she's looking doubtful, maybe puzzled.

"Ahhh," she says.

"What am I talking about?" I says. "I'm mixing up two different friends. Ms. DeJohn lives down the street in another apartment house. My friend what—who— lives in your building is Frank Vollmer."

She tickles the file a little more.

"Oh, yes," she says, the smile growing sunnier. "Here we are."

"He's been there some time," I says.

"Well, two months on a year's lease," she says.

"He tells me how much he likes it. So, anything comes up you'll give me a call?"

She looks at the card on which she wrote down the information I gave her, name, address, et cetera, and says, "You may be assured, Mr. James."

So I leave her office thinking that maybe Connie Di-Bella's mother did raise a stupid child if she's playing around with a prominent person, only a few weeks after she married Joseph DiBella, right in the city where her husband's got eyes and ears, like the late Vincent Pastorelli, all over the place.

27

There's an air of mourning about the late Mrs. Papadopolous's house in Bridgeport. Somebody's hung a
black wreath on the door. You don't see much of that
anymore. I'm wondering if one of the kids O'Meara's
trying to help died or got killed someway out there in
the streets. It's just a small wreath.

I knock on the door and Cora Esper answers it.

"Is there sorrow in the house?" I asks.

"Billy passed away," she says.

"Oh-oh."

I go inside. Some kids are moping around in the living room, watching television with the sound turned
off. They look at me like I'm a stranger, even the
enemy.

I follow Cora down the hall to the kitchen where
O'Meara's at the stove stirring a big pot of soup.

He looks over at me. He makes a motion with his
head toward the box by the heat register where Billy
liked to doze.

Billy's in his box and he looks like he's sleeping. Somebody's covered him up with a blanket like he's a person.

"I'm sorry, Jake."

"Well, he had a good run," he says, but I can see he's not taking it all that easy.

"You told the nieces and nephews yet?"

"I don't want to talk with them people," he says.

"You got to tell the lawyer or at least you got to tell your lawyer, the one who's handling the estate and the trust."

"Well, I'll give it a rest for a day or two."

"I guess that'd be okay. When are you going to bury Billy?"

"This afternoon."

"You got a place?"

"Out in the backyard under the red maple. That's where Mrs. Papadopolous wanted him."

"That's a nice spot," I says, staring out the window at the maple that's showing the light green of new leaves, which'll be a blaze of red like a warm fire come autumn.

"Can you stay?" Cora asks.

"Sure, I can stay."

"You want some soup?" O'Meara asks. "We got plenty. The kids didn't have such big appetites at lunch. Me neither."

"I'll have a little," I says.

I sit down at the kitchen table. It's got new oilcloth on it. I like the smell. I rub my hand on it. It feels good. O'Meara brings me a bowl of soup. There's bread on a platter under a napkin. Cora brings me a clean spoon.

They both sit down and watch me take the first mouthful as though my opinion of it'll mean something.

"Good," I says.

O'Meara nods his head. Cora reaches out and puts her hand on top of his.

"We got practical things to talk about," I says.

"It's all pretty cut and dried, ain't it?" O'Meara says. "I tell the lawyer, he tells the other lawyer who tells the relatives. They tell me to get out."

"Where you going to go?"

"He's coming home with me," Cora says.

"I'm not worried about myself," O'Meara says. He jerks his head, indicating the kids in the living room who are sitting there staring at a silent TV.

"Those people, her nieces and nephews, don't need it. The house. The money," Cora says, like it's so unfair she's ready to scream or weep.

"What people need and what they want is two different things," I says, telling them what they already know. I go into my pocket and bring out the little notebook I carry around. I take out my ballpoint pen.

"I want to make a list; my memory ain't—isn't—so good sometimes."

"Very," Cora says.

"Very what?" I says.

"Very good. Your memory's not very good sometimes."

"Gotcha. So, what I want you to do is give me the names of the relatives again so I can write them down.

Also addresses and telephone numbers if you got them."

"I've got them on the Rolodex," Cora says and gets up to go get it.

Meanwhile O'Meara names them off.

"George Papadopolous, Martin Kalogeras, Mrs. Theresa Bacos, and Mrs. Thelma Argente. Then there's the lawyer, Stanley Duskind. You want that?"

"Well, he ain't really in the picture so far as this idea I want to try is concerned but he's a player, so I might as well talk to him, too."

"What have you got in mind?"

"Well the first thing that came to mind was that I could leave Alfie here to pretend he was Billy as long as you needed him. But that wouldn't be fair to Alfie or the kids you got here or yourself. Besides, I don't mind cutting a corner now and then, if it means giving some black hats a kick in the keister, but being out-and-out dishonest don't appeal to me so I think I'll just try a little friendly persuasion," I says. "I don't guarantee it's going to work, but you remember what Winston Churchill said?"

"It's been a while," O'Meara says.

"He said something like it was better to jaw jaw than war war."

28

When you're facing a situation where you've got to persuade a lot of people to your way of thinking the old idea about divide and conquer ain't a bad idea.

What you got to decide is if you're going to start with the one you figure'll most likely go your way first and work your way up to the toughest nut—sort of like getting your act together or training for the big fight with a few prelims—or maybe you should start with the hardnose because you got to figure if he comes around all the others're going to come around.

I think about that after I get home.

Mary sees I'm being quieter than usual during supper and she asks me what's the matter.

I tell her what's going on over to O'Meara's and how we buried Billy out in the backyard. I tell her I'm going to have to do some talking and I want to give my tongue a little rest because I might be at it quite a while.

"You're going to have these talks tonight?" she asks.

"That's right. The quicker the better," I says.

"It's a school night."

"Well, it's English class and Ms. Esper'll understand because what I'm going to be doing I'm going to be doing for O'Meara which is just as good as doing it for her because they're moving in together. Her place or his, one or the other. Her place if I can't save the house for him and them kids he's trying to get off the streets."

"Are you going to call for appointments to see these nieces and nephews?"

"No, I'm not. I figure it's always better to show up at the door. People know you took a long trip to have a talk with them they ain't—aren't—likely to shut the door in your face."

"I thought that was the curse of being a salesman," Mary says.

I start to say that I ain't a salesman when I see the grin on her face and I says, "I guess you're right, that's what I am, but I still think they'll palm me off if I ask for an appointment a lot quicker than they'll slam the door in my face if I ring the bell." I get up and walk around the table to give her a kiss. "Is it okay I don't help you with the dishes? I'll make it up."

"For heaven's sake, James, I hope we haven't got that kind of marriage."

"I just want to be fair," I says.

She reaches a hand up and grabs my neck and pulls me down for another kiss.

"One thing nobody can ever say about you, Flannery, is that you aren't fair. Who are you going to talk into going your way first?"

"Try to talk into. I ain't—haven't made up my

mind—but it's either going to be George Papadopolous who thinks he's a take-charge kind of guy or Theresa Bacos who's a sugar bun."

"I don't like the sound of that," Mary says, teasing me. "You watch out for sweets."

"You're the only sweet I want," I says, giving her still another kiss, acting silly because part of loving somebody is acting a little silly.

"Why don't you take Alfie with you," Mary says. "He could use an outing."

Alfie hears the word "outing" and is up on his feet running to get his leash off the hook before I can even say yes.

Theresa Bacos and her husband live in a big house over in Ravenswood Gardens which sits on the Chicago River in the Fortieth Ward. He's Greek, and a new Greek Town is growing up over on Western and Lawrence avenues where you can find Greek restaurants, bakeries and food stores. Even so there's been some restaurant closings lately along Lawrence and the Athens, a Greek nightclub on Western, was torn down a couple of years ago.

As I'm parking in front of the two-story white clapboard house—I figure at least four bedrooms, three and a half baths and a formal dining room—I'm wondering what Bacos does for a living. I should've asked. It ain't like me to go into a negotiation like this unprepared, having learned a couple of lessons from old Dunleavy, the boss of Streets and Sanitation, who gets what's practically an FBI dossier on whoever walks through his office door before they start to chat.

"You got to relieve yourself, Alfie?" I asks, who looks at me a little funny because I ain't been talking to him as we drive along like I usually do. He lets me know that it maybe wouldn't be such a bad idea, so I let him out of the car so he can lift his leg on the trunk of this huge shady tree in front of the Bacos house.

I don't notice the front door opening and the next thing I know this voice says, "Do you live around this neighborhood?" and I look up to see a stocky man about fifty standing there under the porch canopy at the top of the stairs.

He's wearing a cardigan sweater and a tie, which tells me he's probably a formal man about things even in his own home.

"Well, no, I ain't—I'm not," I says. "I brought my dog along on this errand I had to run and I just let him out so he could get a little relief."

"Well, that's okay. No reason for the animal to suffer. I just wanted to know if you were local."

He's got a precise way of talking so I think he's probably old country to start with but got his education here. Brought over when he was a kid. These people, I notice, pay special attention to things native born don't bother about.

"Looks like your dog's finished, so you can go do your errand," he says.

"Well, as a matter of fact, the errand I had to run was to come to your house and ask, could I speak to your wife?"

"Oh?" he says, and stands there waiting for more.

"I'm here on behalf of Mr. O'Meara."

"That's the fellow who's living in my wife's aunt's house and takes care of her old dog."

"That's right."

"Come on in, then," he says.

I start to put Alfie back in car but he says, "No need to leave your dog all alone in the car. If it's well behaved there's no reason he shouldn't come in with you."

"Oh, he's very well behaved," I says. "That's very kind of you."

He waves his hand like I shouldn't thank him for a small thing like letting a dog into his house and I notice he's holding on to a napkin, which means I'm disturbing them at their supper.

When Alfie and me reach the top of the stairs, he shakes my hand like I'm an invited guest.

I like this fellow very much even though he's got this formal, standoffish way about him too. I also see he's got soft brown eyes which I think is a good sign.

He directs me through an entry into a very nicely furnished living room with a portrait of his wife and hisself over a spinet piano. It's a little stiff for my taste—like it was moved complete out of a furniture window—not a thing out of place, the tables polished with little crocheted cozies under every vase and porcelain statue, but still it's very nice.

Theresa's standing in the double doorway to the dining room. I can see the table set with white linen and china, crystal glasses and candles which are lighted.

"We're just finishing our dinner. Will you have some dessert and coffee with us?"

"Let me take your topcoat," Bacos says.

All of a sudden I start feeling doubtful about what I'm doing here. Even though I'm on a mission in what I know is a good cause, still and all I'm coming into these people's home with the object in mind of talking them out of something that's rightfully theirs and that, practically any way you look at it, could be called laying down a con.

He shows me into the dining room and directs me to a chair at the dining table.

Theresa finishes clearing the dinner dishes off the table and putting them on the sideboard. She sets down an extra dessert and coffee setting for me and then brings over a cake. The silver coffeepot, creamer and sugar bowl are already on the table.

These people eat like this every night, which is very nice but which is a little too formal for me.

"Cake, Mr. Flannery?" Theresa asks.

"Just coffee. Ever since my wife got pregnant I started putting on a little weight. Now the baby's born and my wife's thin again but I ain't—I'm not—getting rid of it so easy."

"Just a thin slice," she says, and cuts me a little piece which I can hardly refuse. Bacos pours the coffee.

The cake is delicious and I say so.

"We've got very good Greek bakeries just up the block," he says, "but Theresa still prefers to make cakes at home like her aunt taught her."

"Lucky for me. Lucky for you."

He pours me a second cup, then sets the pot down like the social requirements has been satisfied, and looks me in the eye.

"I suppose we might talk about the errand you're running for Mr. O'Meara," he says.

I don't know how to start, so I just say it.

"Billy's dead. The dog O'Meara was taking care of according to Mrs. Bacos's aunt's wishes passed away sometime this morning."

I'm looking at him and looking at her. Tears well up in her eyes. She's a softhearted person.

"We're sorry to hear that," Bacos says. "He was an old dog and had a good life."

"We should all have it as good as that dog," I says. "I have it good and I can see that you have it very good—"

"What are you trying to say, Mr. Flannery?" Bacos says, cutting me off very softly but getting right to the point. Here's a man who deals fair and square but don't waste no—any—time getting to the bottom line.

"O'Meara's been taking care of Billy and living in the house just like Mrs. Papadopolous—God rest her soul—wanted him to do."

Bacos is nodding at me, watching me carefully, waiting for the snapper.

"But that ain't all he's been doing."

"Oh?" they both say, his oh being a little bit suspicious and her oh being just curious.

"You know O'Meara was a cop?" I says.

"Yes, of course," Bacos says. "He had some difficulty and was suspended."

"He had more than a little trouble with the drink and a woman and he was fired without a pension. He was on the skids and the gutter was waiting for him at the bottom when he walked into your aunt's candy store," I says, looking at Theresa more than I look at her husband, letting her know she's the one I'm talking to and she's the one who's going to have to make up her mind about something I'm about to bring up.

"Yes?" she says, in a way that tells me she knows I'm about to ask her for something just like her husband already knows.

"Some people think O'Meara walked into that thief's gun and took three in the belly because he wanted to die. That could be. Who knows? But the thing is, it turned his life around. Your aunt giving him the responsibility of the dog and the house gave him something to live for. It was like therapy for him. It was good medicine and he needed more of it, so he started picking up stray kids off the streets and giving them a place to stay. A bed, and clothes, and warm meals and friends. He gave them like a family."

The Bacoses are glancing at one another while I'm telling them all this like they've had suspicions and conversations about what was going on over at the old house.

"That's a house for a family," Theresa Bacos says.

"What do you think'll happen to the house now that O'Meara's going to have to vacate and turn it over to you and your cousins?"

"According to my aunt's will, the entire estate passes to the four nieces and nephews to be shared out equally."

"I know what that can mean," I says. "I had an old great-aunt who died years ago. The way the relatives fought over the little bits and pieces of what she left could break your heart. It wasn't so much they wanted what they was fighting over, just they didn't want anybody else to get more than what they considered a fair share."

"Perfectly understandable, Mr. Flannery. The greed of one or two will always bring out defensive, even possessive, feelings in others," Bacos says.

"That's right. The really bad part is that certain things that should've stayed with one of the family got sold for next to nothing because there was no way certain things could be divided up. Is that what's going to happen to your aunt's house?"

"I haven't really thought about it," Theresa says.

"That's what will surely happen," her husband says, letting us know that he has thought about it.

"That big house's got a big yard. It's probably on a double lot, maybe even a triple."

"A triple," Bacos says.

"So what'll happen is that grand old house'll get knocked down and some builder's going to stick up three houses in its place. That's the way it'll happen."

Theresa's looking distressed. Bacos is looking at her in a way that tells me that he ain't going to interfere. What she makes up her mind to do is what he'll want her to do.

"I think that old house must mean a lot to you, Mrs. Bacos," I says, "because when you talked about learning how to make this delicious cake, you didn't say your mother taught you—"

"My mother was a good cook—"

"—but that you learned from your aunt."

"—but nothing as good as my aunt."

The memory makes her smile. For a second there she's a little girl again, standing at the big wooden table in the center of her aunt's kitchen, breaking eggs and sifting flour, making a cake.

"What's your proposal, Mr. Flannery?" Bacos asks, getting to the bottom line again.

"I'd like to see that house stay like it is. I'd like to see it used for a halfway house for kids just like O'Meara's doing. I'd like the heirs to take the trust, the stocks and bonds, the cash and whatever, and divvy it up but leave the house to O'Meara."

"There's no love lost between the cousins, do I have to tell you, Mr. Flannery?" Bacos says. "Wait, wait, Theresa, I'm not giving away any family secrets. It's the condition of things and there's no reason why Mr. Flannery shouldn't know what he's facing if he wants to convince all the heirs involved in this matter that they should do a good thing and let Mr. O'Meara keep on helping these children."

I feel a lift in my heart. What he's practically saying is that he knows his wife well enough to know that she's going to say yes to my proposal.

"I wouldn't know what to say to Thelma, George and Martin," she says.

"You don't have to say nothing," I says. "All you got to do is let me tell them that you're for the idea. I'll do the rest. At least I'll do the best I can."

"Which I think, Mr. Flannery, will be considerable," Bacos says. "Will you have another cup of coffee before you go?"

"Well, just half a cup and, if it's okay, could I have another sliver of that cake?"

29

It's getting late but I figure I got time for one more sale. I want to stop by Illinois Masonic to see how Mrs. Vollmer's doing, also on the chance that Frank Vollmer's there with his wife, so that'll take some time and I don't want to be getting home too late.

Theresa Bacos is the niece of old Mrs. Papadopolous's husband. So that's his side of the family. On Mrs. Papadopolous's side of the family you got her sister's son Martin Kalogeras and her brother's two, brother and sister, Thelma Argente and George Papadopolous who I figure is the hardest of the nuts I got to crack.

For one thing he acts like he's the keeper of the family honor and the one who's got to make sure that some banged-up Irish drunk and ex-cop don't end up getting more than he earned or stays in the house a day longer than he's entitled.

O'Meara already told me that George Papadopolous's in real estate which experience tells me makes him a man who'll try to wring every buck he can out of the cock but who'll also be attentive to any kind of tricky negotiation and maneuver what'll—which'll—end up taking a tax or some other advantage out of a property what looks like a loser in today's soft housing market.

If I tackle him and lose, it could mean the end of any chance of O'Meara and his kids staying in the Bridgeport house, but if I tackle him and win, he could bring his sister along without any trouble. Also he lives in the Fortieth, up in the north end of the ward in the Catalpa neighborhood, which ain't very far away and which'll save me driving practically the length of the city all the way to the Nineteenth where the Argentes live.

George and his wife are living in a sensational ranch-style house which looks like it could've been built by Frank Lloyd Wright or at least one of his students.

It's got a long looping drive going up the front entrance but I don't drive up and park by the house in this courtyard which looks like it can accommodate six or seven vehicles not counting the four-car garage off to the side. Instead I park on the street and walk through the open wrought-iron gates and up the path that runs along the brick driveway, knowing that when I passed through I broke the beam of an electric eye. The gates might be open but that don't mean there ain't no security.

I ain't walking up to the front door all that way just for the exercise. You drive up to a rich man's house bold as brass, invading his territory with your ratty old automobile, and he throws his defenses up. You walk with your hat in hand—so to speak—and you've already got him at a disadvantage because he thinks you're at a disadvantage.

I didn't work that out. My old Chinaman, Chips Delvin, explained that to me one time and although I know he likes to make up formulas for success after the fact, some of it makes sense. At least I don't see no reason not to test out such theories now and then.

There's three wide curved brick steps up to the porch and ten yards to the front door which has a huge brass door knocker—the head of a lion—in the middle of it and which opens before I get a chance to put my greasy paws on it and ruin the shine.

A woman in a black dress with white collar and cuffs stands there. She looks a little bit like Mrs. Thimble but, then, I think that Mrs. Thimble looks a little bit like the late Mrs. Banjo, the two housekeepers what Delvin's had in his employ since I know him, and Mrs. Banjo was three times the size of Mrs. Thimble. Sometimes it's the uniform what creates the illusion of alikeness.

"Yes?" she says, and I half expect her to add that I should wipe my feet.

"Let Mr. Flannery in, Mrs. Connely," a man's voice says.

When she opens the door wider I see George Papadopolous standing there in velvet slippers and a cardigan sweater, holding a newspaper in one hand, marking his place with his finger.

He's got a twinkle in his eye and a smile on his face. You don't have to be a mind reader to know he already knows everything I know but even knows exactly why

I'm there. This one ain't going to be that hard, it'll be tricky but not that hard, because a smart aleck what—who—already thinks he's one up on you is really one down.

"Please come in, Mr. Flannery," he says as the house-keeper opens the door even wider to let me slip inside and follow him into the living room. Actually it's what's probably not the living room but what they'd call the library or the study.

There's bookcases lining the walls, a huge antique globe of the world, a collection of leather chairs and couches around a fireplace which has got a fire going in it, though there ain't much of a chill in the air and this house's probably got three furnaces—so the fire's for effect, what you'd call an aesthetic luxury, a coffee table made out of a slab of fossil rock and a beautiful blonde lady sitting underneath a pool of light from a floor lamp who looks up at me like she's been expecting the Duke to arrive for tea.

Papadopolous gives her a look and she slips out of the room before we even get introduced, so that lets me know where I stand in his estimation.

At least he offers me the chair she's been sitting in and takes the chair opposite.

I glance at the fire—he figures he's got all the cards—and says, "You got a cold?"

"What?" he says, caught off guard. "Why do you say that?"

"I just thought, a pretty warm night like tonight, wearing a sweater and with a fire on the grate, you're maybe afraid of catching a little chill."

He gets up out the chair and, staying in a half

crouch, turns off a key in the wall, and the flames die out. It's fake fire which, my way of thinking, don't make it much more than a stage set in a house like this.

When he's back in his chair he says, "Better?"

Now I got to get back in his good graces, so I tell him what I know he already knows.

"Billy passed away today," I says.

"And was buried this afternoon under the old maple," he says, grinning a shark's grin.

I'd make my eyebrows pop up in surprise if I could do it without looking like a monkey, so instead I just go, "Oh, you certainly found that out quick. That's amazing."

"There's not a lot goes on in my aunt's old house that I don't know about. I know, for instance, that he's turned it into a flophouse for drug addicts and child prostitutes."

I wonder how long ago he'd bribed one of the strays into his employ.

"I could differ with you on that," I says, "but we ain't the kind of men to waste time dickering over differences of opinion."

"What kind of men are we?" he says, being a wise guy.

"I'd say we were both men who been successful in their chosen professions."

"Yours is?"

"Politics. The grand old game. And yours is real estate."

"You see a similarity in our careers?"

"We both started from the bottom. You made a fortune in commercial real estate and development. All anybody's got to do is look around to know that."

"I've had a look around where you live," he says. "From the outside," he adds very quick. "I looked over your block with a project in mind not long ago."

I don't believe him for a minute. He looked over where I live to get a handle on the guy who was O'Meara's friend and maybe could give him some inconvenience down the line. That's how far operators like Papadopolous think and plan ahead.

"I hope you decided against trying to buy my building, because it's the heart of my constituency. You know that Hizzoner, the late great, lived in the same neighborhood over to Bridgeport all his life and his son does the same? You stay close to your people. Oh, maybe down the line you get yourself a little place out in the suburbs, out in the country, but you never give up your base."

"Which contributed to your success," he says, like he's finishing my case for me.

"That's right. I'm the committeeman of the Twenty-seventh now."

"I thought the Machine's been dead for a number of years, ever since the wreck of the 1968 Democratic convention."

"Then—you'll excuse my saying so—you ain't been paying attention. A statement like the one you just made, coming from a man into commercial real estate development, working out there with Dunleavy over to Streets and Sanitation, going through the building permit process, looking around for targets of opportunity—"

"Opportunity?" he says, showing a little interest.

"—like the municipal contracts given out by Municipal Pier, Canal, Garages, Public Curbs and Expansion Agency of which a friend of mine—my teacher as a matter of fact—Frank Vollmer is the chairman."

We let that sit there like a sugarplum on that chunk of fossil rock with the impression of the bodies of animals what lived a million years ago in it, pretending I didn't say anything that even vaguely resembles an offer. Which I didn't but which he thinks I did.

"I live where I live because it's going to help me when I decide to run for alderman and maybe who knows what else, just like you live where you live because it helps your image in what you do," I says, picking up that thread again, making like we're both a couple of schemers doing what we do for all the right reasons . . . money and power.

"I haven't offered you a drink, Mr. Flannery," he says, like it just that second dawned on him that he's got a drink near his hand but I got nothing.

"Nothing, thanks," I says.

He looks around for something to offer me so that it'll be that he offered the hospitality of his house and I accepted the hospitality of his house. He picks up a candy dish filled with hard candies wrapped in fancy paper.

"Please," he says.

I take a candy. "For later," I says.

"Take a few. They're imported."

I take a couple more and put them in my pocket. Now he thinks he's created a friendly atmosphere and settles back.

"You came to see me about something to do with dear old Billy and Mr. O'Meara?" he says.

"Well, you told me what you think he's doing with them kids—"

"No, no—" he says, waving his hand.

"—he's taking in off the streets."

"—I was being too harsh. I'm sure he's trying to help those unfortunate children."

"That's good, because that's exactly what he's trying to do."

"What are you hoping to get from me?" he asks.

"The house."

"Well, now . . ." he says, tilting his head and smiling like that's asking a lot.

"Not for O'Meara to keep and do with whatever he wants. Put into a trust. A home for stray kids, halfway house."

"You'd need permits and permissions from the neighbors to make that legal and official," he points out.

"I know the ins and outs of that," I says. "That'll be my contribution to the cause."

"That's a valuable property," he says.

"Not so valuable as it was, say, a year, two years ago. What we got is a soft real estate market around Chicago, around the whole country."

"A market correction. It'll pick up again when the economy picks up."

"I've got no doubt. So you hold back on the actual giving of the property into the trust until things improve. Meanwhile you give O'Meara an irrevocable hold on the land. The thing is you'll have this big

asset sitting there waiting for you to use it as a contribution and a deduction whenever your tax situation
makes such a donation most beneficial to you. Meanwhile you take the depreciation against a rental of one
dollar a year land rent."

"You seem to know a lot about such dealings."

He rings a buzzer, and Mrs. Connely pops up in the
doorway like a jack-in-the-box.

"Would you ask Mrs. Papadopolous to join us in
about five minutes?" Papadopolous says.

When Mrs. Connely pops out, I pick up the conversation.

"Politics is my profession and such dealings—
among other things—is my business," I says.

"How about maintenance of the property before and
after it's put into trust?"

"That's also my obligation. We pay the operating
costs through fund-raisers which I am very good at or-
ganizing."

"I'll bet you are, Mr. Flannery," he says, giving me
the old one-eye, like he knows that I'm the kind of
hairpin what skims ten, twenty percent all the time off
any fund-raiser I organize and endorse.

"So the bulk of the estate, except for that old house,
comes to the heirs, you and your cousins, to divvy up
any way you decide to divvy it up."

"Equal shares," he says.

"After the expenses of administering the estate," I
says, letting him know I know there's ways of slicing
off a couple of hams while the pig's on the way to the
slaughterhouse.

There we are, he thinks, a couple of shrewd operators, cutting up the pie, trading more than favors, trading deals and money.

"The proposal sounds very good to me, Mr. Flannery."

"I thought you'd like it."

"I can make the case to my sister. She'll see the advantages to the arrangement immediately. My cousin Theresa and my cousin Martin might have less reason to find it attractive."

"Well, I already talked to Mrs. Bacos and she's all for it."

"Oh?"

"I made out what a good and charitable thing it would be to do."

"Yes, I can see you're going to go far, Mr. Flannery."

"Call me Jimmy, Mr. Papadopolous. Practically everybody does," I says.

"And please call me George, Jimmy," he says. "Very few people do."

Mrs. Papadopolous breezes into the room then, looking wide-eyed, obedient, socially useful and expectant.

Papadopolous and me—I—stand up. He gives us an introduction. She holds out her hand and I shake it. It's very smooth and cool. We sit down and make a little polite chat about this and that. She offers me a candy from the dish. I take a few more and everybody's happy.

30

Joan Vollmer ain't in her room at Illinois Masonic. I go up to the nurses' station and ask this big African-American lady does she know what happened to the patient in that room; did she wake up or didn't she?

"Are you a relative?" she asks.

"I never could understand that," I says. "Whenever I ask about the condition of a patient—on the phone or in person like I'm doing now, hospital workers—everybody—always ask am I a relative. Which means I got a choice if I ain't a relative but only a concerned friend. I can say I ain't and come up empty or I can lie and say I'm a brother, a cousin, whatever, and get the news. What would you do if I said I was Mrs. Vollmer's brother, ask for identification?"

"I'd ask you how come you don't call your sister by her first name," she says.

"I'm very interested in Joan's welfare," I says. "If you could be so kind, you could at least tell me if she's still alive."

"As far as the record shows she's alive, recovering and out of here."

"When did she wake up?"

She waves a finger at me. "That's all you get," she says.

"Is Ms. Klein in her office?"

"You're just going to have to go and see," she says.

So that's what I do.

Sylvia Klein's working late, which I got an idea she does a lot more often than she goes home on time.

"What can I do for you?" she asks.

"We've never met, but I hear a lot about you from my wife."

"You must be Jimmy Flannery," she says, sticking out her hand for a shake, "and I hear a lot about you. Not only from Mary but here and there. Your fame precedes you."

"Oh?" I says, not knowing should I be flattered or otherwise.

"Take a load off your feet," she says. "You want a Coke or a coffee?"

"I'd just like a little news."

"Don't ask me to break patient confidentiality."

"I just want to know is Mrs. Vollmer okay."

"She became fully conscious early this morning."

"Was her husband called?"

"I'm sure he would have been."

"But you don't know if he showed up to see her."

"I wasn't here at one o'clock in the morning when she woke up asking for something to eat."

"How do you know—"

"I was told by the head nurse on duty when I came

on board at seven o'clock this morning," she says before I can finish my question. "When I take over the
supervision of staff each day I get reports from every
ward, room and facility except for surgery and ER.

"Mrs. Vollmer woke around one. You'd be surprised
how dramatic that awakening can be. Out like a light
one minute, raring to go the next, except for a little
weakness from being in bed for such a long stretch.
She woke up complaining about the bladder catheter
and about being hungry. The catheter was removed
and she used the toilet. They brought her something
to eat. Hot cereal, toast and tea."

"Was her doctor called?"

"Immediately. He'd left orders to be informed the
moment she awakened."

"How long before he arrived?"

She sighs, gets up and goes to the file. She pulls out
a folder and comes back to sit down behind her desk.

"We're walking the line here, Flannery," she says.

"If my reputation's preceded me, like you say, then
you know that I ain't being nosey just for the fun of it.
I've got good reasons for wanting to know."

"Like what?"

"Like Frank Vollmer, your patient's husband, could
be missing."

"No, he's not. He came to take her home."

"That's written down there?"

"No, it's written up here," she says, tapping herself
on the head with her finger. "I was present."

"You mind giving me the details starting back with
the doctor's arrival?"

She stares at me. Maybe it's something in my voice

or the way I'm sitting on the edge of the chair without hardly knowing I'm doing it, trying to persuade her to give me information I'm not entitled to have.

"Is somebody in danger here?" she asks.

"I don't know enough to give you a definite yes, but I know enough to give you a definite maybe."

"Dr. Goldner was informed of Mrs. Vollmer's awakening at oh-one-twenty-two—one twenty-two A.M. He arrived at oh-one-fifty-five—"

"Almost two A.M.," I says, so she won't go on translating military time—which hospitals use for accuracy—into everyday time like everybody uses.

"He examined Mrs. Vollmer. Her pulse and blood pressure were within normal parameters. She seemed completely recovered. Dr. Goldner remained with her for over an hour. Hey!"

"Hey, what?"

"Dr. Goldner wasn't the admitting physician. That was a Dr. Breedlove."

"You know either one of these doctors?"

"I know Dr. Breedlove personally."

She taps some keys on her word processor, and in a second a screen comes up which lists the doctors what got—who have—admitting privileges at Illinois Masonic.

"Dr. Goldner has admitting privileges."

"How come nobody noticed the doctor who came to see her when she woke up wasn't the same one who admitted her?"

"The change of physicians was authorized."

"Is this Goldner a specialist?"

"He's an internist."

"How about Breedlove?"

"Also an internist and family practitioner."

"So, why the switch?"

"It could be Breedlove was going off on a vacation or Mr. Vollmer had asked for a second opinion or took Breedlove off the case altogether."

"Why would he do that?"

"Don't ask me to read minds. You'll have to ask Mr. Vollmer."

"When did he arrive?"

"According to the record, Dr. Goldner left around three twenty," she says, giving it to me the ordinary way, "and was back at seven thirty in the morning to sign her out."

"He signed her out, or Vollmer signed her out?"

"Dr. Goldner released her. Mr. Vollmer arrived with two other men just before Dr. Goldner showed up at seven thirty. He had a small suitcase with Mrs. Vollmer's clothes and makeup case in it."

"How do you—"

"I was there. I was there to see that there were no delays or misunderstandings. Mr. Vollmer and Dr. Goldner had called in advance to make sure there'd be none."

"These two men with Frank Vollmer, what'd they look like?"

"They were big men. Well dressed."

"Were they carrying?"

"You mean were they armed?"

"Maybe you noticed they held their arms like they was carrying something under an armpit?"

"How would I know something like that?"

"Well, I just thought—hoped. A lot of detectives must come through here and I thought maybe it'd registered once upon a time that a man carrying a gun in a shoulder holster carries hisself in a certain way."

She frowns, thinking about it, but she finally shakes her head and says, "I can't swear to anything like that."

"So they took Mrs. Vollmer out of here in a car?"

"In an ambulance. They were still treating her like glass though the doctor clearly wanted her back in a home environment."

"Would it be all right if I asked your drivers where they took her?"

"It wasn't one of our ambulances. It was a private service."

"You happen to remember which one?"

"Carstairs. You need an address?"

"It'll save me a minute or two, thank you very much," I says.

She taps the keys again and comes up with another screen. She jots down the address and telephone number of the private ambulance service on a note pad, tears off the page, folds it and hands it to me with a smile.

"Say hello to Mary for me," she says.

"I'm going home right now and do that," I says, and thank her again. "You know, anytime you need a favor all you got to do is call."

"That's what people say about you, Mr. Flannery."

"Call me Jimmy," I says, and I leave.

Alfie's sleeping on the passenger's seat when I get into the car. It's past his bedtime. He don't look pleased that I woke him up but he yawns, stretches and tries to look interested when I start talking it out.

I review everything I know or think I know. He gives me another yawn when I give him a look as I pull up at a traffic light.

My mouth's very dry. I take out a piece of the hard candy George Papadopolous offered me and start to unwrap it. It tastes vaguely of soap. I look at the wrapper to make sure I don't accept a piece of candy of that brand again. It's imported stuff from Italy called Dolce Firenze.

I know Firenze means Florence. Then I remember that Dolce means sweet. Sweet Florence or Florence Sweets, depending on how Italian grammar works.

The light changes. I'm still sitting there thinking. Somebody honks the horn behind me and I start moving while I'm remembering what Mrs. Vollmer said to me when she come out of the fog for that little minute the other night. "Dolce" she said. Sweet or sweets. That's the nickname they give Bruno. I can't swear that an idea can hit you like a light bulb going on over the head of a character in a cartoon, but that's what it feels like.

I also think I hear a bunch of clicking noises which—I swear—is pieces of a story falling into place.

31

I got to talk the ideas I got swimming around in my head out with somebody.

Alfie's a very good listener but he don't contribute much from the other end; he don't ask any questions and he don't suggest any maybes.

My father's a newly married man and although he's a man who'll have plenty of questions and alternatives, I think what I need is somebody a little less active and a little more judicial.

Anything that has anything to do with our lives together, I talk over with Mary, but, just like most cops I know, when the things I get involved in look like they could maybe get a little dangerous and telling her about them would give her too much distress, I tend to keep it to myself. I ain't saying that's the right thing to do, especially nowadays when women want things to be even-Steven all the way around, but I just can't give up the notion that I should save the person I love the most any unnecessary grief or worry any time I can.

So what that leaves me with is my old Chinaman, Delvin, except I notice lately that his solution to practically anything is Butt out.

In the end I call Vellitri's private number and ask for an interview which he graciously extends to me.

This time I drive myself over to his house. This time a woman opens the door and shows me into the old warlord's library. This time Ginger and Finks ain't even around.

"Sit down, Jimmy," he says, half rising from his chair by the fire and I says, "Don't get up, please, Mr. Vellitri," and he waves his hand and says, "No, no. Call me Vito," and I sit down and says, "Thank you, Vito."

Without him even ordering it, the woman—it could be his housekeeper, it could be his sister—comes in with two espressos on a tray, Vellitri's usual gesture of hospitality.

He takes a sip and makes a face, half amused at hisself, half annoyed with hisself.

"My last habit. My last vice. The booze, the cigars, the women have all lost their savor. Only the strong coffee pleases me anymore. Can you believe it, my doctor tells me I drink too much of the stuff. It's burning a hole in my stomach. Ah, so what?"

I take a sip of mine.

"It's very good," I says.

"That's what I'm saying," he says. "So, how can I be of service?"

"I need your counsel and advice."

He smiles and says, "You make me sound like a godfather. I never been a godfather, except to the little children of friends and relatives, of course."

"I understand. Still and all, I thought about all the wise people I know and, in this situation, I decided you were the wisest."

"I'm gratified," he says and waves his hand, which is the pale, waxy hand of a prince of the church, telling me to state the case.

When I don't get right to it, he gives me a look.

"You hesitate," he says.

"I'm afraid I might offend you."

"Does what troubles you touch upon me and mine?"

"Upon friendships and associations."

"Then, having told me of your awareness, begin and let me be the judge of the propriety. I'll stop you if you go too far."

"When we discussed this business of the DiBellas and the Vollmers the last time we met, you gave me a very good idea of the character of the men and women involved."

He nods.

"Now I want to go a little deeper. I'd like you to tell me if a story I invented could explain certain things."

"A story?" he says.

"A possibility," I says.

"There's no harm in stories as long as they aren't necessarily to be believed."

"The way my story goes is this head of a very large organization decides to retire and return to the place where he was born, leaving his chair at the head of the corporation table vacant.

"There's three vice presidents could take the spot. The oldest one should've been a shoo-in but he takes on a young wife and that maybe looks like he ain't as steady and dependable as could be desired. Of the two young V.P.s one's a rough and ready type, more likely to try intimidation than negotiation, coercion than persuasion, and the other one's very smart, very smooth, but maybe not as decisive as he could be, maybe can't handle himself as good in the clinches. Who knows?

"There's the possibility of a very important deal involving this important and influential head of a municipal agency that's suddenly got a lot of plums to hand out, and the retiring CEO decides that's a good way to test the talents of these three V.P.s."

"How each one goes about acquiring this lucrative contract or series of contracts," Vellitri says, letting me know that he's following me.

"So the oldest man, the one with the young wife, throws her at this man of influence."

"He trades the virtue of his wife for an advantage with this man?" Vellitri says, outraged at the notion of such a thing.

"I don't know what encourages an old man to take a young woman for a wife. There could be a lot of passion, sure—"

"But not in great or enduring measure?" Vellitri says.

"—but, like you just said, that could fade pretty fast. Also a young wife is something to show off, a possession to be proud of, something to make young men full of envy and—if the game was worth it—something to use to your advantage."

"It's possible. Morality has changed."

"So it happens the way the older executive wants it to happen. His young wife seduces the man of influence and the husband now has the lever to move the man of influence this way and that way."

"Joseph DiBella has Frank Vollmer in his pocket," Vellitri says. It's clear he's as tired of all this *Godfather* One, Two and Three way of telling the story as I'm getting to be.

"That's the idea," I says. "Bruno Falduto ain't about to send his bride-to-be into the same kind of action. He does it the other way around. He goes out and tells Mrs. Vollmer that her husband's allowed hisself to be compromised."

"Figuring what?"

"Figuring the wife'll blow the whistle and cause a scandal. Figuring that the bad publicity'll be enough to get Vollmer tossed off the Municipal Pier, Canal, Garages, Public Curbs and Expansion Agency, which will toss a wrench into the spokes of his uncle's wheel."

"But none of that comes out."

"Because Bruno Falduto, who's soon going be married to Angelina Donato in a very big wedding to be held in Sicily and paid for by the big man, Carmine DiBella hisself, sees this pale, blonde, porcelain doll what belongs to Frank Vollmer, and he gets an appetite. Maybe he thinks of it as a sort of last shot at the buffet before he puts hisself on a diet of home cooking."

"Young men and women," Vellitri says, shaking his head at the power of the hormones that lead us around by our noses when we're young.

"Bruno Falduto is a very smooth and good-looking man. He gets a hunger with the ladies, I don't think he's got any trouble satisfying it, especially if he's got an angle. With Mrs. Vollmer, he's got a very good angle. He convinces her she should get a little back from Frank, the quickest way possible. He convinces her that 'What's sauce for the gander is sauce for the goose' ain't a bad way to do it."

"Which leaves Anthony DiBella out in the cold with nothing to toss into the pot—"

"Except threat of mayhem. He takes the short way. He has Frank Vollmer picked up and held. He picks up Vollmer's wife when Vollmer hangs tough."

"You think he's got them both?"

"I'd bet on it, but you could make a call and make sure."

"Call who?"

I hand him the slip of paper with the number of the Carstairs Private Ambulance Service on it.

He punches up the number on the telephone on the table next to his chair.

"She was taken from Illinois Masonic this morning. All we want to know is where they took her. If they took her home, my story's probably just a story."

"Hello," Vellitri says. "My name is John Enderby. I just got into town to see my sister, Mrs. Frank Vollmer, who was hospitalized at Illinois Masonic, but it seems she was released this morning and was taken away in one of your ambulances. I'm at the hospital now and I'd like to know where she was taken."

He listens as the speaker on the other end gives him what he wants to know. He don't bother writing down whatever he's being told.

He hangs up and rubs his hands together. They whisper like dry paper. He stands up.

"I think we should leave right away and visit Anthony DiBella. Ginger and Finks will drive us."

"I'm very grateful for your support," I says, getting to my feet, "but, you don't mind my asking, why are you walking this extra mile with me?"

"Jimmy, Jimmy, Jimmy," Vellitri says, pleased that he's got me puzzled, "who do you think Carmine DiBella asked to be the judge of the performances of the men who would be his successor?"

32

We're driving along in silence, me and Vellitri in the back, Ginger and Finks up front.

Just before we get to Anthony DiBella's mansion, Vellitri says to me, "What do you think put Vollmer's wife into the hospital?"

"I don't know. It could be she felt bad about what she done with Bruno and tried to kill herself in a fit of remorse."

"It'd be more likely she'd try to off the husband," Vellitri says.

Up front Ginger and Finks keep quiet but nod their heads in agreement.

"Or it could be Frank Vollmer tried to do it to her," I says.

"To do what? Run away with Connie DiBella? Very unlikely," Vellitri says.

Ginger and Finks nod again.

"Which leaves us with what?" I asks.

"Which leaves us with another thing we'll have to

settle," Vellitri says as we stop at the gate. "One thing you've got to always remember. Never jump in with both feet until you've got all the facts."

Ginger and Finks give each other a look, like they're checking to see if men of action like themselves can profit from that advice.

Ginger, who's driving, pushes the speaker button. It squawks, asking who wants in, and when Ginger says "Vito Vellitri" the gates swing open and we drive up to the front door.

By the time we get there, Joseph and Anthony Di-Bella, and Bruno Falduto, and some of their lieutenants and *consiglieres* are all out in front with big smiles on their faces ready to give the old politician the big Italian welcome—big hugs, kisses on both cheeks and all like that.

There's a half a dozen foot soldiers standing around in the background eyeing up Ginger and Finks.

They're the only ones acting like there's any chance for trouble, which I guess is all right, because that's what they get paid for.

For a minute there I wonder if they're going to pat us down, but this is not a rival gang boss visiting the stronghold of other gang bosses. This is an old politician, a power in the city and the Italian community, related to some by blood, to others by marriage, a man who can walk everywhere in safety.

They call him "Uncle" and "Grandfather" in Italian and he accepts it all, doing a number on them, making himself look even more fragile and harmless than he really is, the master negotiator at work.

"We talk," he says.

Inside the house there's all of a sudden servants and female relatives running all over the place bringing food and drink.

"You all know Jimmy Flannery, a friend of mine, a fellow committeeman, recently took over the Twenty-seventh from my old friend Delvin."

Everybody shakes my hand, even Anthony who I can see don't like me and Bruno, who don't like me but doesn't show it.

"I'd like to talk to Frank Vollmer," Vellitri says, and holds up his hand immediately like he don't want anybody to try lying to him.

Joseph DiBella looks at Connie, his wife, who's like hanging around in the background, staying out of the way of the men but ready to serve them if anything's wanted.

"Connie, will you find Frank and ask him to join us?"

She trots out. We grin at each other and make a lot of small talk about how bad crime is getting in the city what with the new immigrants, the Asiatic gangs, the black gangs and the Hispanic gangs. These sons and grandsons and nephews of the immigrants from the old country, the Jews, the Irish and the Italians, who were the gangsters of the twenties and thirties. These heirs of violence who still keep their hand into prostitution, hijacking, gambling, drugs, a little of this and little of that, but who mostly make their millions on vigorish from loan-sharking and lobbying with bribes and occasional threats for the commercial laundry business, the garbage collection and the construction contracts of the big town.

Frank Vollmer comes strolling in wearing one of his hundred-dollar shirts, two-hundred-dollar pairs of pants, four-hundred-dollar pairs of shoes and another five-hundred-dollar sweater. He's got a drink in his hand and he don't look any the worse for wear.

"Hello, Jimmy," he says. "Are you keeping well, Vito?"

"We came to see how you were doing," Vellitri says.

"I'm doing very well," Vollmer says, his eyebrows popping up like he's very surprised anybody should think he wasn't.

"Well, it looked like you fell off the face of the earth for more than a couple of days here. Nobody knew where you was. Not your—"

"I had a lot of thinking to do—"

"—housekeeper, not your office."

"—and I needed to be alone to do it."

"Thinking about the contracts you'll be giving out as chairman of the Municipal Pier, Canal, Garages, Public Curbs and Expansion Agency?" I says.

"I just make recommendations. I wanted to think about that, yes."

"Some people would say this ain't exactly neutral territory. I mean it's well known that most of the gentlemen here have an interest in construction companies, one way or another," I says.

"I've been listening to proposals, yes," Vollmer says. "But that wasn't the primary reason for my coming here."

"What was the primary reason?" I asks.

"My wife's been ill, as you know. I wanted her out of the hospital because I don't think a hospital is the best place for a person to get over an illness. I was going to take my wife to a resort, but my friends offered her a quiet place to stay in a beautiful setting. Have you seen the gardens?"

"I got beautiful gardens," Anthony says in a voice like gravel falling out of a truck.

I'm wondering if Vollmer really did try to kill his wife. I'm wondering if part of the deal he's cutting here is that the DiBellas and Falduto should take care of that little problem for him.

"If you'd like to go out and see the gardens," Vollmer says, "you could say hello to Joan."

I start to say that I'll see the gardens and Joan after a while, but I catch a look from the corner of my eye and I understand that Vellitri's telling me to leave the room if I want a chance at finding out what's really going down here, because these Italians ain't about to talk business in front of me.

So I go out through these huge French doors and across a slate patio about half the size of the block I live on and down some steps into a garden which is—like they said—just beautiful. There's a path leading to a fountain which is sparkling in the sunlight. There's a white wicker garden set beside the fountain and someone laying on the chaise with a lap robe thrown over her legs.

I walk up and Joan Vollmer don't stir. I stand there looking down at her, thinking what a pretty woman she is. She was even pretty when she was unconscious; now, with more color in her cheeks, she's a knockout. She opens her eyes and smiles at me, lifting a hand because I'm standing with the sun behind me and I'm probably lost in the glare.

I move around and sit down where she don't have to shade her eyes.

She frowns a little bit. "Do I know you? I feel as though I've seen you before."

"Well, we never been introduced, but I came to visit you in the hospital and you opened your eyes for a couple of seconds and then you went back to sleep."

"Why?" she says.

"Why what?"

"Why did you come to visit me?"

"I'm a student in your husband's night school class. I was concerned."

"What's your name?"

"Jimmy Flannery."

"I've heard of you. Where have I heard of you?"

"My name's been in the papers and on television a couple of times."

"Oh, yes, I remember something about a gorilla."

She's remembering the time I had something to do with Baby, the gorilla in the Lincoln Park Zoo what is the city's pet.

"Did you come to visit me just because you're a student in my husband's night school class?"

"I had a stronger interest than that."

She don't ask me what. I can see she's a woman what—who—can read a lot in people's faces, who can put two and two together without a lot of information.

"What is it you want to know, Mr. Flannery?"

"You can tell me it's none of my business—"

"I know that."

"—but I'd like to know how you landed in the hospital."

"You have suspicions that Frank wanted me out of the way."

"That's putting it on the line."

"Why not put it on the line? You know plenty or you wouldn't be here."

"Okay."

"Frank didn't spike my hot chocolate. I didn't try to take the Dutch cure," she says, which means commit suicide.

"Hey, I ain't heard that since the last time my old man said it."

"My old man used to say it too," she says. "So, we've got something in common."

"Looks like it."

"Which means you've got to believe it's the truth when I tell you it's the truth."

"I'd say so."

"I had more to drink than I was used to. I took a Valium and an aspirin. I was obviously pretty confused because it looks like I kept on taking one or the other every five minutes or so because I'd forget I took any at all. Someplace along the way I was overdosed and the next thing I knew . . ." She waves a hand, letting me fill in the coma and the hospital and what came after.

"One more question?" I asks.

She nods.

"What're you doing here?"

"Beats the hell out of me. What I think is a bunch of syndicate types, Mafia types, whatever types thought having me and Frank here would give them some leverage."

"Is it working?"

"What do you think?"

"Well, I don't really know. I ain't been around."

"Use your head, Jimmy. Connie DiBella had a waltz with Frank and Bruno Falduto had a waltz with me and since Anthony couldn't offer either one of us an interesting partner, all he could do was try to steal a dance by force. So, now, they're talking about share and share alike on the new contracts Municipal Pier, Canal, Garages, Public Curbs and Expansion will be giving out. Isn't that the way you figure they'd figure?"

"The thing none of them knows is that they figured wrong. They went through all this trouble for nothing."

"Oh?" she says. "Don't tell me. I don't want to know."

I shake her hand and walk back along the path and up the steps and across the patio into the living room. The second Vellitri sees me, he gets up from his chair.

Everybody rushes around asking him to stay but he says he'll be on his way if Frank Vollmer will be so kind as to show him to the door.

The three of us walk out with Ginger and Finks in front a distance and the rest of the crowd staying well back.

Vellitri puts his hand on Frank Vollmer's arm.

"Jimmy," he says, "our friend, Frank, here, tells me how much he enjoys teaching. He tells me he wants to do more of it. That will mean cutting back on other

duties. He'll be resigning as chairman of the Municipal Pier, Canal, Garages, Public Curbs and Expansion
Agency. Isn't that right, Frank?"

"I'd like it better if I could be officially removed."

"I understand. We can arrange that, can't we,
Jimmy?"

"Happy to," I says.

"So, you're off the hook all the way around," Vellitri
says.

We're walking across the porch and down the steps
to the car. Ginger and Finks are opening the doors.
The DiBellas and Faldutos are gathered on the porch
watching the old man who was to be their judge in the
competition arranged by Carmine DiBella walk away.

"I don't know about is he off the hook," I says.

"What do you mean, Jimmy?" Vellitri asks, tight-
ening his grip on Frank's arm, telling him to shut up.

"There's the killing of Vincent Pastorelli," I says.

"I didn't kill him. I panicked. She sent me a note
demanding to see me that night or else. I didn't know
that Joseph was setting me up with Connie. It was an
accident. I swear it was an accident."

"He was run over twice, not once."

"The car got away from me. It jumped the curb and
got away. I swear it."

"Are you satisfied, Jimmy?" Vellitri asks.

"No, I'm not satisfied," I says.

Vellitri smiles. "But Joseph DiBella is satisfied.
Frank would have had to be more than just convincing
to satisfy Joseph about the death of an old friend. I
think we can depend on the thoroughness with which
he looked into the matter."

Vellitri lets go of Frank. Vollmer steps back. Finks helps the old warlord into the limousine. I go around and get in the other side. Ginger don't help me. He gets behind the wheel. Finks gets into the front passenger seat. We start driving away. Vellitri leans forward and raises his hand like a prince of the church giving all the losers a blessing. Or maybe he was giving them the finger.

33

A couple of things about most people. They expect perfect justice even though they know there ain't no—any—such thing.

Walking away with nothing but Frank Vollmer's word that he didn't actually set out to kill Vince Pastorelli maybe don't look like justice. But the way you got to figure it, he's been humiliated by Connie Di-Bella using him the way she did and Bruno Falduto using his wife, Joan, the way he did. Everybody using everybody the way they done. Frank and Joan got something to work out there. Probably they don't, so he loses a lot right there. Not to mention the chair of Municipal Pier, Canal, Garages, Public Curbs and Expansion, which you can bet was the platform from which he intended to launch a political career. He'll have to put that idea away for a while.

The executives of what was once Carmine DiBella's Family ain't going to get a shot at any city contracts in the near future. The word goes out they lost some of their clout and that does even more damage. Not that they're going to be out there selling apples or pencils in the street and living in cardboard boxes, but they're going to learn they ain't got the power which they thought they had.

So, what I'm saying, you got to be satisfied with less than perfect justice. You got to be satisfied with what you can get most of the time, it don't matter if we're talking reward or punishment.

I got one more thing I got to try and clear up. I got to go have a talk with the last of Mrs. Papadopolous's relatives.

Martin Kalogeras lives in a duplex over in the Thirty-sixth, which is the most Italian ward in the city ever since so many of them was displaced when the Chicago Circle campus, now the University of Illinois at Chicago, was constructed back in the sixties.

It don't look like Martin's done as good financially as his cousins.

I ring the bell and after a couple of minutes a man opens the door. He's in his undershirt and he's wearing old-fashioned carpet slippers. He's got a very open face when he smiles at me, a different person than the one I met over to the house.

"Can I help you?" he asks.

"My name's Jimmy Flannery."

"Oh, sure. I remember you. That was a nice gag with whatever you had on that rubber glove when you shook everybody's hand," he says, like he's about to laugh.

"What stuff?" I says, giving him a big grin so he knows I knows he knows.

"What's a man doing running around with rubber gloves on his hands unless there was something on the gloves he didn't want to get on his skin?"

"I could've had a rash."

"Okay, you could've," he says while he's walking up the stairs and I'm following.

It's a nice comfortable apartment he shows me into. It looks a lot like the one in which me and Mary live, right down to the playpen with a little bouncer in it sitting in the middle of the living room.

"I got one about that age," I says.

"I got five more just like it, different sizes. They're all in bed."

A very pretty Italian woman walks into the room and I understand how come the Greek's living in an Italian neighborhood. Because his wife wants it, probably because her family lives all around her.

He introduces me to Felitia.

"Would you like some biscotti and hot chocolate?" she asks.

I'm about to pat my waistline and refuse, except in this house I know how important the giving and taking of hospitality is, so I say I'd be pleased.

"Sit down," Kalogeras says, as Felitia leaves the room. "I already got the word about your scheme."

"It ain't a scheme. There's nothing in it for me."

"But something in it for your friend O'Meara and his sweetie. Hey, I ain't unsympathetic. I always thought my aunt should've turned the house over to O'Meara and that old dog in the first place. Now, it's a little more complicated."

"What do you mean?"

"Well, now O'Meara's got to set up a nonprofit foundation, do all that paperwork, pay for the lawyer's expenses—maybe we can help him out a little with that—before we can turn the property over to him. Otherwise it has to be appraised and added to the bulk of the estate which'll put it way over the six-hundred-thousand-dollar exemption allowed against taxes."

"You seem to know your onions," I says.

"I do a little real estate. Nothing big. Just a little rental here, a triplex there. I'm putting enough away for our old age, when it rolls around, and for our kids, to give them a start when they grow up."

Felitia comes back with the hot chocolate and biscotti which she tells me she bakes herself.

"My relatives want to live in their money. That's all right. But we don't need luxury. Comfort suits us very nicely."

Felitia nods and smiles and asks me to have another biscotto.

"What did you promise George?" Kalogeras asks.

"Not a thing."

"You didn't even give him a hint there'd be some privilege forthcoming? He let something slip about city contracts."

"I don't do things that way. I can be a little tricky when I got to, but I very rarely come right out and lie."

"So, okay, George's having pipe dreams as usual. Well, you get O'Meara to set up his nonprofit and get a lawyer to make out the deed of transfer. You know what to do?"

"I can handle it."

"Disappointed?" he asks.

"Disappointed about what?"

"About how you didn't get a chance to tell your story and weave your spell. Did I make it too easy for you?"

"I like it easy when I can get it," I says.

"Have another biscotto," Felitia says.

I'm full as a goat when I leave the Kalogeras flat.

I decide to stop over to Delvin's before going home. Don't ask me why. Maybe because Kalogeras was right and I had this story I wanted to tell, a prize to win with this silver tongue which I'm beginning to think I really got—a thing which I better watch out for because that's how certain kinds of politicians get to be full of themselves—I got nobody to listen to me brag.

Mrs. Thimble lets me in and shows me into Delvin's parlor.

He's in his easy chair, reading.

He looks at me over his glasses and says, "Ah, Jimmy, have you come to crow?"

"You know about what happened with O'Meara and the house?"

"I was talking about Vollmer and DiBella's crumbling empire."

"Vellitri called?"

"He called to tell me to urge you to be discreet. 'Let sleeping Sicilians lie' is the way he put it."

I tell him about the way these men used and abused their women.

He hears me out, his head thrown back, his eyes half closed in that thoughtful way Pat O'Brien had when he played a priest on those old movies on the late-late show.

When I'm through, Delvin takes a pull on his whiskey and says, "You ever know Hickey Boyle?"

"Was a committeeman over to the Forty-second?"

"The Twelfth. Anyways, he finds out that his wife's having a go with the neighbor while Hickey's out there tending to business. This happens a couple of years ago when them home television cameras first come out. So Hickey goes down and buys hisself one of them cameras and a shotgun. After he makes a big thing about not coming home till late because he's got to go over to the capitol in Springfield, he goes back home in the middle of the afternoon and goes creeping up the stairs, throws open the door to the bedroom and shouts, 'Aha!' There they was in bed, his wife and the neighbor."

"Naked?"

"In the fifth position. The wife sees Hickey and she's so scared she clamps down on her boyfriend's head. Nearly crushes his jaw. Hickey starts taking pictures for evidence. He wants to make sure she don't get a cent out of him when he tosses her out and divorces her."

"I can understand that," I says.

"Hickey's pushing on the camera button, keeping them from running out of the room with the threat of the shotgun, but the camera won't work. Fran—that's

Hickey's wife—gets up and starts running out of the room. Hickey grabs her and throws her back on the bed. This guy she's with, the next-door neighbor, Harry Bognelli—you know Harry Bognelli?"

"No, I'm afraid I never had the pleasure," I says.

"He's into sanitary fill? Owns a dump over in Lake County? There's a possibility he could be dumping hazardous waste illegally over there?"

"I don't think so."

"You don't think he's dumping hazardous waste?"

"I mean, from your description, I don't think I know this Harry Bognelli."

"Well, I always thought he was an okay guy. I met him once or twice when Hickey invited me over for a meal. Hickey and Bognelli used to do barbecue together, being next-door neighbors and all. I guess that's how it starts."

"Doing barbecue?"

"You know what I mean. Everybody lounging around in bathing suits and shorts all day. It's got to stir the blood."

He smiles, remembering the days when such sights stirred his blood. Sweet remembering.

"So, the television camera?" I says, reminding him about where he is in his story which, I got to admit, has already got me hooked.

"He just bought it, you understand, and Hickey's not the best in the world working gadgets in the first place. But he figures he's finally got the camera ready. He's still threatening them with the shotgun. He hits the camera button and the damn camera still won't work. Fran jumps out of bed again and heads for the

door. Hickey chases after her, grabs her by the arm at
the top of the stairs, drags her back into the bedroom
and tosses her into bed with Harry again. He tries to
work the camera the third time, but it's still a no go.
It makes Hickey so goddamn mad, that camera not
working, that he fires the shotgun into the air and
blows a hole in his own roof."

"Anybody get hurt?"

"Well, a piece of plaster conked Bognelli on the
head. Nothing serious."

"So nobody got wounded?"

"Except Hickey, Jim. He was wounded in his heart,
his wife cheating on him like that and blowing a hole
in his own roof which is a very expensive item to get
repaired nowadays."

"How did the story get out?" I asks.

"Hickey told it to me in person."

"How come he told a story like that on himself?"

"He wanted to know if I knew a good roofer who
was available and would work cheap or maybe needed
a favor Hickey could do him."

"He didn't know a roofer in his own ward?"

"Sure he knew roofers in his own ward, but he was
trying to keep the story quiet in his own neighborhood."

I was confused, but that's not unusual when Delvin
tells me a story in order to make a point, which I
sometimes got to dig for.

"So, how come he thought he had to tell you the
story if all he wanted was the name of a roofer?" I asks.

"Because he wanted to tell the truth to somebody he
respected but wasn't too dear a friend."

"How's that?"

"Because acquaintances don't often become enemies, but friends do. And they'll use whatever you told them in confidence against you. That's the sad truth."

"But why did he want to tell anybody the truth at all?"

"Because he had a girlfriend he was keeping in a flat Back of the Yards. In case I already knew it, he was whitewashing hisself. His wife gave him an excuse and a reason for cheating on her. You understand what I'm saying? Like Mrs. Vollmer. Hickey didn't really want to cheat on his wife, but he did because she did and that's how come he blew a hole in his roof."

"That's a pretty twisty story," I says.

"Life's pretty twisty," he says, staring off into the past.

He's slipped through one of the folds in time that old people slip through every now and then.

Then he shakes himself, leans forward with some effort and peers at me.

"You could use a drink to celebrate your victory," he says. "Mrs. Thimble won't refuse a guest."

"I got to tell you," I says, lowering my voice confidentially, "I think Mrs. Thimble knows I don't drink liquor."

"But she won't admit it. You understand? If she admitted it, she couldn't feel smug about knowing I'm a liar and a cheat."

We been through this same conversation or one very much like it three or four times the last couple of weeks and I know there's going to be a lot more of it, his memory bouncing around like the little ball that used to bounce around on the words at the singalongs in the movie houses way back when.

So I call for a toddy, which Mrs. Thimble brings and which Delvin snatches from my hand before her back is hardly turned.

As I'm about to leave Delvin says, "Hey, Jimmy, one more thing. Take Vellitri's advice. Remember, curiosity killed the cat."

"It never killed you," I says.

He tips his drink to me and smiles.